Who is Alice Weaver? The CIA believes they are about to find out...but are they? Do they really want to meet the real Alice Weaver? Perhaps, some things are better left hidden. Some agents think they already know who Alice is. After all, they have a file on her and so does the FBI. But what they know is only what Alice wants them to know. When Alice Weaver shares information with those in authority, they will be left scrambling for cover!

A K'Anne Meinel novel

Also by K'Anne Meinel:

Novels in Paperback:

SHIPS *CompanionSHIP, FriendSHIP,*
RelationSHIP
Long Distance Romance
Children of Another Mother
Erotica
The Claim
Bikini's Are Dangerous
The Complete Series
Germanic
Malice Masterpieces 1
The First Five Books
Represented
Timed Romance
Malice Masterpieces 2
Books Six through Ten
The Journey Home
Out at the Inn
Shorts
Anthology Volume 1
Lawyered
Malice Masterpieces 3
Books Eleven through Fifteen
Blown Away
Blown Away
The Alternate Cover

Small Town Angel
Pirated Love
Doctored
Veil of Silence
Malice Masterpieces 4
Books Sixteen through Twenty
The Outsider
Pirated Heart
Recombinant Love
Survivors
Inn the Dog House
Flight
An Island Between Us
Malice Masterpieces 5
Books Twenty-One through Twenty-Five
Malice Masterpieces 6
Books Twenty-Six through Thirty
Beauty and the Beast

Vetted Series:
Vetted
Cavalcade (Prequel)
Pioneering (Prequel)
Vetted Further
Vetted Again

Novellas in Paperback:

Sapphic Surfer
Sapphic Cowgirl
Sapphic Cowboi
Sayyida
The Northwood Lodge

The Malice Series:
Mysterious Malice (Book 1)
Meticulous Malice (Book 2)
Mistaken Malice (Book 3)
Malicious Malice (Book 4)
Masterful Malice (Book 5)
Matrimonial Malice (Book 6)
Mourning Malice (Book 7)
Murderous Malice (Book 8)
Mental Malice (Book 9)
Menacing Malice (Book 10)
Minor Malice (Book 11)
Morally Malice (Book 12)
Morose Malice (Book 13)
Melancholy Malice (Book 14)

Mad Malice (Book 15)
Macabre Malice (Book 16)
Marinating Malice (Book 17)
Macerating Malice (Book 18)
Minacious Malice (Book 19)
Meddlesome Malice (Book 20)
Meandering Malice (Book 21)
Maniacal Malice (Book 22)
Monitoring Malice (Book 23)
Marked Malice (Book 24)
Mandating Malice (Book 25)
Methodical Malice (Book 26)
Malevolent Malice (Book 27)
Militarial Malice (Book 28)
Machiavellian Malice (Book 29)
Malefic Malice (Book 30)

Religious Experience
Lied

All Novels and Novellas in paperback are also available as e-books.

Novellas in Paperback Continued:

A Woman Down Under Series:
Shanghaied (Prequel)
Outback Born
Outback Bred
Outback Heritage

Outback Native
Outback Splendor
Outback Yearnings (Prequel)
Outback Escape

Pocket Paperbacks:

Mysterious Malice (Book 1)
Sapphic Surfer
Sapphic Cowgirl
Meticulous Malice (Book 2)
Mistaken Malice (Book 3)
Malicious Malice (Book 4)
Masterful Malice (Book 5)
Matrimonial Malice (Book 6)
Mourning Malice (Book 7)
Murderous Malice (Book 8)

Mental Malice (Book 9)
Menacing Malice (Book 10)
Minor Malice (Book 11)
Morally Malice (Book 12)
Morose Malice (Book 13)
Melancholy Malice (Book 14)
Mad Malice (Book 15)
Macabre Malice (Book 16)
Marinating Malice (Book 17)

In E-Book Format:
Short Stories

Fantasy
Wet & Wet Again
Family Night
Quickie ~ Against the Car
Quickie ~ Against the Wall
Quickie ~ Over the Couch
Mile High Club
Quickie ~ Under the Pier
Heel or Heal
Kiss
Family Night 2
Beach Dreams
Internet Dreamers
Snoggered

On the Parkway
Stable Affair
Kept
Stolen
Agitated
Love of my LIFE
Quickie in an Elevator,
GOING DOWN?
Into the Garden
The Book Case
The Other Women
Menage a WHAT?

LARGE Print Novels

SHIPS CompanionSHIP, FriendSHIP,
RelationSHIP
Erotica Volume 1
Long Distance Romance
Children of Another Mother
Bikini's Are Dangerous
The Complete Series

Malice Masterpieces
The First Five Books
To Love a Shooting Star
The Claim
Represented
Timed Romance

K'ANNE MEINEL

Mandating

Malice

ISBN-13: 978-1959436010

K'Anne Meinel is available for comments at KAnneMeinel@aim.com as well as on Facebook, Google +, or her blog @ http://kannemeinel.wordpress.com/ or on Twitter @ kannemeinelaim.com, or on her website @ www.kannemeinel.com if you would like to follow her to find out about stories and book's releases.

www.shadoepublishing.com

ShadoePublishing@gmail.com

Shadoe Publishing is a United States of America company
Cover by: K'Anne Meinel
Edited by: Deb Amia

Mandating Malice

PUBLISHER'S NOTE

MANDATING MALICE

Book 25

"A deal, ma'am?" he asked respectfully and cautiously. They got a lot of crazies in here thinking they had valuable information on UFOs or neighbors who must be spies from another country because of their accents. People didn't realize exactly what the CIA did, but since so much of it was covert, people assumed the agency would want to learn their secrets. As the first line of defense in this building, he had to screen everyone.

"Yes. Is Madelyn Korbel in?" she asked pleasantly.

The man looked at her, relaxing marginally. She was dressed nicely, and that alone had him judging her as *not* one of the crazies. Plus, she was asking for a senior person within the hierarchy that made up the agency, so

she either knew something, or someone had given her the name to help her get past this first level of security. "Your name?" he asked officiously.

"Alice Weaver," she told him and had her identification ready. It was the new card issued by the state of California. It was brand spanking new and shiny. It had only recently been reissued when they confirmed she was indeed alive. They had reinstated her driver's license with a horrible picture showing her emaciated face and punk rock hairstyle. She had frequently thought the identification she had forged or had forged for her over the years was better than anything the state issued. She'd even started to round out a little since this picture was taken.

"Wait here, ma'am?" he said as he scanned her ID and handed it back to her, looking at her inquiringly and watching her behavior surreptitiously as he reached for a phone.

Alice nodded, looking curiously about as people came and went within the large atrium. It looked like everyone was conducting important business from all the suits she could see. She kept herself quiet and breathed slowly to still her hammering heart. Was she anxious? Yes, that must be it. She wasn't anxious for what she was about to reveal but for her family and what could happen to them. She was taking a gamble, but she had gambled all her life. Mostly, she had won, but occasionally, she had failed, and that wasn't an option she took lightly.

* * * * *

"Someone is asking for Madelyn Korbel? By *name*?" a voice asked into the phone, shocked and becoming concerned. No one asked for her anymore. He listened for a moment before nodding and hanging up the phone after saying, "I'll be right there." As soon as his phone

disconnected, he made another phone call, going up the chain of command. When his call was answered, he said, "Someone is in the lobby asking for Madelyn Korbel." He listened, nodded a couple of times as though the speaker could see him, and said, "Yes, sir. I'll see what I can find out."

Alice was superficially aware when someone exited the elevators at the far end of the atrium. Another suit. He hurried up to the reception desk where several uniformed guards were busily doing their jobs, but he specifically approached the guard she had spoken with. By body language alone, it seemed obvious they were trying to talk about her without giving themselves away. They failed. Alice was very aware she was under surveillance. Anyone who entered this establishment was watched, and the name she had so innocently asked about was one she knew would produce results. She glanced at the obvious cameras in the lobby trained on this guard station. She wondered idly how many cameras there were that she couldn't see.

"Ms. Weaver?" the man approached her, and Alice pretended to turn in surprise. She'd watched them out of the corners of her amazing eyes, very aware of her surroundings.

He was holding out his hand to shake hers, and she took it, noting that it was soft, so he must not do much manual labor. The handshake was firm, and she responded in kind, assessing the man now that he was up close. "I'm Stewart Commons," he told her. "You were asking for Madelyn Korbel?"

"Yes, I was. Is she available?" she answered pleasantly, releasing his hand. She was pleased that his palm hadn't been damp or his hold on her hand too long.

"I'm sorry, Madelyn Korbel has retired. Is there something I could help you with?" He was assessing her just as the security officer had. She was dressed nicely, not too corporate, but she looked…powerful was the only word he could think to express himself, but that word was inadequate. There was something about her he couldn't put his finger on, something he sensed due to his training over the years. He'd think more about it later.

"Are you her replacement?" she asked, surprised to find that Madelyn had retired. Alice thought that woman would have died at her desk before she left. Then she had a thought, *Either Madelyn was testing her, feeling her out to see what she really wanted, or they had forcibly retired her.* That sounded plausible. The woman was a legend.

Stewart chuckled and shook his head. "No one could replace Madelyn. What was it you wanted to see her about?"

"Mr. Commons," she said, and her tone suggested she didn't believe that was his real name, "Let's not play the social niceties game. Neither of us has the time. By now, my name is raising certain flags within your agency. It will raise further flags in the FBI databases you share. The redactions in my file alone should tell you and your people that I don't just drop in for tea or a friendly visit with an old friend. Let's get Madelyn or her replacement, and let's see if the information I have is useful to you and your people, shall we?" her voice was cordial, polite even, but at the same time, it was commanding, and he found himself compelled to do exactly what she asked but stopped himself.

"Ms…Weaver, I have to know what you are here to see Madelyn about before we can proceed."

"Ah, I see. You are going to play the games associated with your level of clearance, which you seem destined to remain at," she said, exasperated already and not willing to be too polite with this hireling. This really was

a matter of some urgency. She sighed. "I have information regarding arms shipments in Kazakhstan and Russia, and I'm certain that anyone who pulls up my files will see I'm not bluffing. Your obviously inadequate security clearance makes it impossible for me to divulge further information, so trot back to your superiors and tell them I would like to make a deal. And if you can't produce Madelyn, I suggest her replacement or a superior be coughed up pretty quickly, because my patience is going to run out if I'm only given subordinates to deal with."

He was shocked and surprised to be referred to as a subordinate and insulted that his security clearance wasn't high enough to deal with this. His eyes betrayed his annoyance, but Alice wasn't perturbed in the least. She tended to rub people the wrong way...often deliberately. People in this line of work judged on appearances. She was aware of that and had picked out this pantsuit accordingly. It fit her better than any of her older clothes, which would have hung on her reduced frame. At least, this one appeared fitted for her. She felt confident in it, which would help her maintain her cool through what she was certain would be a long day or two.

Without saying a word to her, he nodded stiffly and walked away, murmuring to security to, "Watch her," which they would have done anyway. Alice made herself comfortable on a bench. She knew the wait wouldn't be too long, but she wanted to watch the atrium while she sat. She knew there had to be dozens of cameras trained on anyone entering the building, but she was certain several would now be analyzing her, making sure she matched whatever outdated photographs they had on her.

* * * * *

Two days ago, Alice had been answering the officer's questions about the nearly fatal encounter with Special Agent Linda Miller. This officer had been at the scene for what had been the first of three questionings their family had been put through. After the first session, Alice had called Portia, not only to get her perspective on the situation but to hand her Linda's phone and download the files on it. Breaking the phone's security code had been a simple matter of learning Linda's birthdate and entering it backwards. Not too concerned with security on her personal phone, it had taken a mere half hour for Alice to figure out the code, so they could download the files to Portia's computer. Since Alice's household computers and her children's personal computers had been confiscated by the IRS, she couldn't use any of the fancy programs she normally had access to. After finding the most important file on the agent's phone—her recording that proved she was not hiding behind her badge—Alice sent it to herself in the form of an email. The remaining files she placed into a file she created on Portia's computer to use in her defense because she knew this wasn't over, not by a long shot. The call history, Linda's contacts, even her photos and text message screen captures, were sent to Alice's email address but only when Portia wasn't looking. Alice quickly erased the history on Portia's email and computer, so she wouldn't be aware of what Alice had done, hoping if Portia's computer were compromised, it might not show up easily. She wished she had her own computers, so she could overwrite her actions and prevent whoever was investigating her from discovering what she'd done, several times if necessary.

The second interview with a lieutenant from Linda's precinct didn't go as smoothly as the first. He was a little suspicious, perhaps also a little homophobic, and he took in the expensive Palos Verdes estate with

distaste. Officially giving him Linda's phone, which they claimed to have found after the other officer had taken away Linda's badge, gun, and jacket, didn't seem to faze him the same way.

"Have you seen what is on here?" he asked suspiciously, holding up the cell phone.

"As you can see, it's locked," Alice replied and saw from the corner of her eye when Portia shifted uncomfortably. It was a telltale sign to Alice, but the lawyer was out of the officer's line of sight and only listening in to protect her client's interests, just in case. Alice gave the appearance she was answering his questions but was doing her best not to.

"Were you aware of Agent Miller's interest in your wife?" he asked.

"Of course. My wife was free to date when she thought me deceased, and she informed me when I returned." *I also watched the entire failed courtship*, she felt like adding but refrained.

"You weren't jealous? You didn't want revenge?"

"Of course, I was jealous. I love my wife. However, the logical side of me," she nearly laughed at this statement but refrained from making the situation worse, "says she didn't know I was alive and was free to pursue other arrangements."

"You were getting a divorce before you disappeared?"

"We were estranged when I disappeared but hadn't started divorce proceedings," she corrected tightly, the only sign of her annoyance as his questions became increasingly personal. They continued like this for half an hour, and Portia only interjected twice: once, when he asked about the IRS, which was none of his business and had nothing to do with his investigation into the behavior of his agent, and the second time, when he warned Alice not to go anywhere.

"Are you saying my client is under suspicion of something?"

"Well, we do have to get Agent Miller's side of things," he tried to say reasonably but forcefully, and Alice deliberately looked at the lawyer. Was this guy in on whatever Linda had been looking into? Was he aware of her extra-curricular activities?

"You'll let us know?" Portia asked dismissively, a cue for the lieutenant to leave.

"Of course," he said charmingly while rising. "If you think of anything else, please let me know," he added as he dropped his card on the coffee table.

"Think you'll get the recording off that?" Alice asked innocently, gesturing at the mobile phone.

"I'm sure we will," he assured her as he slipped it in his pocket.

"Wanna bet that phone disappears?" Alice murmured to Portia as he drove away.

"You think he'd tamper with evidence?" she asked, shocked.

Alice looked at their family friend. She had known this woman for decades, and it still amazed her how naive the attorney could be. She didn't answer, her sardonic look and raised eyebrow saying it all.

* * * * *

Alice looked at her cell phone to check the time. They'd kept her waiting an hour already. There were several calls from Kathy on her phone, but she hadn't heard them because she'd turned off the sound. She glanced at security and saw them watching her to see if she was going to use her phone, so they could either report her or ask her to put it away. She had no intention of answering Kathy or anyone else's calls right now. She had a specific agenda, and the time spent here had been allotted in her

carefully-made plans. She thought back to what had happened the day after she sent Linda to the hospital....

* * * * *

The IRS had turned up at the end of their driveway, flashing badges and demanding they be let into the estate. They had officially *served* Alice and Kathy Weaver for bank fraud, tax fraud, and failing to report a foreign bank account as well as tax evasion, grand larceny, and finally, criminal liability. The document implied they could stay in their home for the time being but that was pending as the case wound through the court system. The clear threat was they were about to be arrested, and yet, they didn't arrest them, which was suspicious given the charges being leveled. Alice was genuinely surprised they weren't being evicted based on the charges before them; however, the good ole American system of justice made the IRS comply, and they would have to wend their way through the courts. The family's eviction and the selling of their estate, which the IRS would confiscate for unpaid taxes, was the ultimate goal and would come in time.

"Oh, my God, Alice! What are we going to do?" Kathy asked, panicked as she read through the charges.

"I'll handle it," she tried to reassure her wife.

"But what can you do? They seem pretty sure they have a case." Kathy sounded like she was going to cry, and it irked Alice that her wife didn't have more faith in her abilities. Just then, the phone rang, and Kathy went to answer it. Apparently, Andi and Portia had been served at their office at the same time. They would learn a while later that their accountant and tax firms had been served as well.

"Someone seems to have a hard-on for us," Alice murmured thoughtfully as she began to formulate her plan of action. This two-pronged attack that *seemed* unrelated was too unrelated not to *be* related.

"Where are you going?" Kathy asked as Alice put on a jacket.

"You don't mind if I drive your Lexus, do you?" Alice asked as she grabbed the keys off the hook.

"Don't you think I should go with you?"

"The kids are going to be frightened if those bozos come back," she pointed out, not being clear if she meant the IRS agents who had tacked official notices at the end of their driveway on the gate as well as on the front door or the police investigating Linda's accident at their house. Alice had torn the notices down, seeing no need to advertise their personal business to their neighbors.

The third police interview had been rather tense when the lieutenant returned with another officer, this one from the Palos Verdes police department. Alice now knew who had been on the other end of the tapes that had been transcribed; she recognized the name from her computer files. And so did Kathy, whose poker face could use some work. "I need to check the computers," she said in a low voice, so only Kathy could hear. "I want to check them," she lied cheerfully, knowing Kathy wanted to be in on this as a true and equal partner. Kathy didn't like that she couldn't know everything, and Alice had already started working out a plan to leave her family in peace.

Alice shook her tail after getting on the freeway, backtracking enough to ensure she was no longer being followed. She parked at the car park and got into her sedan, first checking in on the computers as she had told her wife and then heading to a rental counter where she rented a Porsche. She sighed in relief to be driving one of the familiar, expensive sports cars

again. It further helped to disguise her when she stopped to buy some clothes. She got several outfits that fit her better than her old clothes and were even better than the things she had purchased in Dubai.

She approached a house in the expensive Los Angeles suburb of Trousdale Estates, located in an exclusive Beverly Hills' community in the foothills of the Santa Monica mountains. She looked up at those mountains, feeling the cold and wondering if they would get snow on them this year. Was it colder today, or was that just her imagination? She had been in their heated pool just yesterday. *Wow! Yesterday seemed a lifetime ago*, she thought as she pressed the button at the gate, her Porsche being scrutinized by the security camera.

"Can I help you?" the voice came through the tin box.

"I'm here to see Sebastian."

"Who are you?"

"Alice Weaver."

There was a delay of several moments before the voice continued with, "Alice Weaver is dead."

"I assure you, I am not," she replied, wanting to laugh.

"Sebastian can't see you," the voice answered with finality.

Alice sighed. Did Sebastian not want to see her, or was this a ploy? She knew she scared him as well as excited him. This was one of several homes he owned, which she had found over the years, and she knew he hated that she was so easily able to find him. However, he had given up long ago trying to figure out how she found him. His enemies couldn't find him, so how could Alice?

Well, she had tried the diplomatic approach. Now, she was going to have to get dirty, and that wasn't something she relished. She backed the Porsche away from the gate and considered ramming it—after all, she had

taken out some rather expensive insurance on the over-priced sports car—but she reconsidered. She didn't want to start with hostilities, and those around Sebastian tended to have automatic machine guns. She parked the Porsche in the next neighborhood, which was saying something about the distance, with these little estates. It reminded her of her own Palos Verdes estate, but her view was better as she looked onto the ocean instead of Los Angeles.

She slid off her impractical but stylish shoes, replacing them with black sports shoes. She zipped up a matching, black sports jacket and slicked her fingers through her spiky hair, wondering if it would grow faster someday, although she did like the ease of caring for it these days. She walked down the street, appearing to the casual observer as a lonely jogger on a midday run. She searched for and figured out which were the walls to Sebastian's estate. Noting that one of his neighbors was leaving as she approached the gate, she slipped between it before it could close, so she could follow his wall and leap up to swing over the eight-foot fence using a branch to facilitate her boost. It had been a scramble, and she was grateful there was no razor wire or broken glass on the top to keep out intruders. She looked over the area for a while, saw where the guards and cameras were, and ascertained a blind spot which she didn't hesitate to use, slipping into it to get within feet of the house before she had to duck and pry open a window. The window creaked from disuse, but she got inside. Breathing hard, she wondered if she would ever get back in the shape she had been. Kazakhstan, Russia, and Central America, while she'd been on the go and active, had been the culmination of a lot of hard times, and her body was still recovering slowly, from that emaciation.

Haltingly, she moved through the unfamiliar house, looking for alarms or triggers that would give away her presence. She saw the library and

was headed for it but veered away when a well-dressed man headed upstairs with a tray. Curious, she slipped from the shadows, watching for laser lights that would have set off any alarms and rapidly following his footsteps up the stairs in time to see him slip into a double-doored room. She slipped into the room next door to it and looked around. She saw it was empty and put her ear to the wall first, and then against a door. She was hearing a rumbling of voices, one of which she thought she recognized as Sebastian's, but it had been so long and perhaps she was mistaken. Something about what she was hearing felt off, and this disturbed her. She waited until she heard the door in the next room open and shut, then let a little time pass before she left the room she was hiding in and headed for what she was sure was the master bedroom.

"Sebastian?" she asked, shocked to see the condition her old friend was in. He was lying in bed and looked just as emaciated as she had been, only he also had a flushed face and his customarily impeccably trimmed beard was looking unkempt. The normally large, robust man was a fraction of what he had been. She looked around the darkened room with its drapes drawn and saw the medicines on the side tables and the tray of food across his lap.

He stared hard at her, not believing his own eyes. She was dead! If Alice was coming to take him on to Valhalla though, he couldn't have asked for a better escort. Damn, she was thin. What happened to those amazing breasts and the curves he had often lusted after? "Alice?" he asked in a slightly raspy voice, unsure. He wasn't sure he shouldn't be terrified. She had meant death to many people over the years.

She smiled, showing even and very white teeth. Was it his imagination, or were the eye teeth a little longer than necessary? Was she now a vampire? Surely, it was his imagination. Yes, that was it, the

medications were off. "I come to visit my old friend only to find him in bed. Are you ill?" she asked, knowing the answer before he even answered. Her eyes didn't lie.

"Cancer," he growled, sounding winded.

"Damn!" she exclaimed. "I am sorry, my friend. I won't bother you. I hope you get better and soon."

"Wait, don't leave!" he stopped her with his request. "You can't possibly know what this visit means to me, my friend. When I heard you were dead…" he began and then thought again. "I went to your memorial and gave my regards to your widow. I should have known…no corpse, no Alice," he chuckled at his sally. "What can I do for you?"

"Sebastian, really. I wouldn't think of asking for a favor…" she began, knowing he wasn't up to the task she had intended to ask.

"I am still in charge," he insisted, sounding a little like the Sebastian of old. "Dammit, don't write me off yet. Those bastards are already thinking they can divvy up my belongings," he lamented angrily, gesturing out the bedroom door and towards the downstairs. "At least, you bring some excitement. There is an honesty I cannot compare. No one is like the great Alice Weaver. I can see your death was greatly exaggerated, although, you didn't come away unscathed." At her nod, he smiled, but it was a mere caricature of the former man. "I believe I am still in your debt for some diamonds you left with me. What can I do for you, my friend?"

"I would like to hire some of your men and women. I need them to be invisible, and I want some of your best weaponless fighters."

"Of course. You have a job that needs this expertise?" he asked, sounding excited at the prospect of ordering his people around.

She nodded. "I need them to guard my family," she said simply.

His eyes took on a speculative look. "You won't be there?"

"Your people can disappear *if* I return home."

"If?"

She nodded, not going into details. She waited. He waited. When the waiting became unbearable, he cleared his throat and nodded. "I can let you have four. Will that be enough?"

"Thank you, Sebastian. You must let me pay you...."

He shook his head. The hair on his head had thinned to an alarming degree, its blackness making it look stringy, and were those grey hairs? "No, Alice. This may be my last order, but I give it gladly. You have made my life interesting a few times," he laughed, ending in a coughing fit that caused him to hock up something in a fine, linen napkin from the tray. He hadn't eaten much; he wasn't that hungry.

Alice waited respectfully, waiting for him to get his breath back. She admired the art above his fireplace mantle, the room warm and cozy and not in need of a fire.

"Need I ask how you found this hideout of mine?" he asked finally. She always found him, even when he didn't want to be found.

Alice turned back, a grin on her face. Her eyes were glittering, and he laughed again as he shook his head. "You'd be a better bloodhound than my enemies. I wish..." he began but left off. They both knew what he wished. He had tried to recruit Alice years ago. It hadn't gone well. He had not only tried to recruit her but also seduce her. She broke all his limbs for his impertinence and persistence, and he'd been laid up for months. She had visited him faithfully every week, feeding him chocolates and bringing him sweet and exotic-smelling oils that could be rubbed on his aching limbs until they healed. He had been in one of their safe houses, locked from the inside, and still, she managed to appear frequently, in a different spot in the house or sometimes, a different house.

They never did figure out how she had done that. It was then, he determined she was a better friend than an enemy. It had been a very profitable friendship over the years.

His mind, usually wandering because of his illness, medications, and boredom, remembered when someone had asked if she had special training and he attempted to find out. The men he had sent to find this information for him had come up missing. The fourth one had appeared in his bed with blood leaking from every orifice. There was no sign of struggle, and it had been a definite warning. He'd been in another safe house that time too.

Alice was one amazing woman, and he had regrets, but he had been younger and in the prime of his life. He had never thought his strength would fail him, but the cancer had been insidious. He wasn't sure going out in a blaze of gunfire wouldn't have been a better option. The pain was…well, it was more than he had expected. He cleared his throat and asked, "How is your family? The kids okay?"

She smiled again, looking proud. "The younger ones are teenagers now."

He winced, realizing the passage of time. He'd remembered Alice when she was single and with no sign of marriage in sight. He wouldn't have thought someone like her would have dared because it made her vulnerable. With her skills, he would have thought she'd…still, she looked happy. He envied her that since he had missed finding happiness in his own life. "Anyone in particular coming after them?" he asked suddenly, all business again.

"IRS and apparently, the cops."

"You want us to shoot it out with them?"

She immediately shook her head. "No, but if it looks like they are going to take the house, I want you to get my family out. Get them onto a

private plane south of the border with enough gas to get them to South America. Kathy will know where to go from there. Just make sure she has a few thousand cash to play with."

He nodded. Kathy would have every luxury, if he had to do it himself, and he would. It might kill him to do so, but for Alice Weaver he'd do it. "Anything else?"

She shook her head. "Anything I can do for you?" she asked, then turned as the door opened and a man and a woman entered. She stepped back into the shadows but not before she was seen. Dammit! She should have heard them coming. Sebastian's carpets were rich and deep, and she'd been concerned for her friend, so she'd missed the sound of their approach.

The man reached for a gun, and that was his mistake. Alice took him down, almost reflexively, and when he tried to fight her, she broke his arm. The exertion was a bit much for her, much to her surprise, but she triumphed, and she froze when she was confronted by the woman.

"No," a now weak Sebastian tried to stop the inevitable violence. The man, his bodyguard, had been taken unawares, and it was natural that he reached for a gun, but he didn't know Alice Weaver. Sebastian was shocked when Alice stood there, just staring at the woman. "Do you know each other?" he asked, breaking the silence as both women seemed equally startled to find the other there.

"She's my neighbor," the woman told him, suddenly shaking slightly.

"That's right," Alice said, not sure she could lie her way out of this one. Since Sandi had found her in Sebastian's bedroom, it was fair to assume she was involved in something illegal, and then Alice remembered that Sandi was a hospice nurse. She glanced at Sebastian. Maybe her presence was legitimate; he did not look well.

"Alice is a business acquaintance. She used to invest money for me and came by to see how I was doing."

"Ugh," the man on the floor was moaning, holding his broken arm.

"I suggest you go get that fixed," Alice told him conversationally. "And I'd leave that gun alone or I'll shove it up your–" she started to add but glancing at Sandi, rethought it. Nothing like impressing the neighbors.

Two other men, having heard the commotion, came running into the room. Seeing Alice, they went for her. She crouched, preparing for their attack, but Sebastian croaked, "No!" Holding up his hand, he pointed and added, "Take him out of here, and see to his arm. You can go too, Sandi."

"You need your meds now that you have eaten," she contradicted.

"I have not eaten. I've been discussing old times with Alice. I'll call you when I'm done," he said meaningfully, "so you can tell me which meds I need."

Sandi took the hint, glancing curiously at Alice Weaver. She would have never thought to find her here. She hesitated only a moment, used to arguing with this difficult patient and not wishing to lose the upper hand. Then, seeing Alice watching her, those disturbing cat-like eyes on her, she decided to leave. She left the door open, and Alice followed to make sure no one was outside the door before gently closing it and returning to stand near Sebastian as he gestured from his bed.

"She's killing me," he stated boldly.

"Are you sure?" It confirmed something Alice had seen in the woman's eyes the first time she met her.

He nodded. "I think she gets joy from it, but I'm not sure what she's using. I'm dying by degrees, and I don't know how to tell. She's a sadist."

Alice added to the mental file she had started on Sandi and Richard Pasternack. "Let me guess…someone in Russia recommended her?"

"How in the world did you know that?" He was astounded by the things she just seemed to *know*. She was always miles ahead of everyone else.

Something clicked for Alice. She didn't answer Sebastian. "Is Richard handling your portfolio or banking for you?"

He nodded warily, wondering what she knew.

"You can bet you won't live to see your ill-gotten gains, and those moneys are probably back in Russia now. Do you have a will?"

He nodded but looked entirely floored by her knowledge of his finances and personnel.

"It's not going to mean diddly when they get done with you. There won't be anything left. Want me to do you a favor?" she asked, feeling the old impulses rising through her pores.

"No," he said, surprising her. "I transferred the funds a long time ago. I have no children, and the aunts and uncles who benefited got that benefit long ago. I sold most of my assets, but they don't know that. When the doctor gave me my terminal diagnosis and recommended hospice care, I took his recommendation, and the Pasternacks came into my life. The little they have seen and have handled isn't nearly as much as they think I have. Convenient, eh?"

She nodded, wondering at this new mystery but knowing the result would be the same.

He started to cough again, took a sip of water from the glass on his side table, and began again. "I see it in her eyes. She's enjoying the pain I'm in and what she is doing to me."

Alice nodded again. It confirmed once again what she herself had seen in Sandi's eyes. Someday, she'd do something about that, but right now, she had other things to take care of. "Is she causing you additional pain?" she asked. Had he been standing up, he would have taken a step back, but as it was, he cringed slightly at the look on her face…those eyes!

"No, no pain from her, but she enjoys making me feel helpless, and these drugs…" his hands took in the many medications, "some have no effect until I wake many hours or maybe days later. She's killing me slowly and enjoying every minute of it. I thought you were a ghost come to take me to Valhalla when I saw you," he laughed, making an odd sound as he gasped for breath. This was the most he had spoken in a while as he waited to die. He wanted to die in his own bed in comfort. The thought of going out in a blaze of bullets was a young man's bravado.

"Wouldn't be a bad way to go, eh?" she asked softly, knowing of his attraction for her for so many years.

"We've both gotten older. Well, you got better, and I just got old," he acknowledged. He leaned over and pressed a button on the side table. "I pay my debts," he promised.

Alice stood by as the same two men returned to the room, looking at her curiously.

"This woman needs your expertise. She needs four people to watch her home in shifts. *Quietly.* No guns and no violence unless necessary. You pick the four," he said, addressing the older of the two men. "I want absolute discretion." Alice fidgeted, and Sebastian saw it. "Something to add?"

"They should look like they belong in Palos Verdes," she added, seeing the younger man wearing a sports track suit that looked like it belonged at

a Good Guy's reunion with its zipper down the front. It screamed mafia wannabe.

Sebastian nodded, and the older man he was addressing nodded. "Where?"

Alice gave him the address and added, "It's my wife and kids. The IRS and the Palos Verdes' cops are watching. I'm going to rattle some cages, and I don't know who might come for them. If that happens, I want you to get them out of there. They can't see your people–"

Sebastian interrupted, "Have my jet gassed and ready in case it's needed to take them to South America. Mrs. Weaver, Kathy, will tell you where to take her when the time is right…if it comes to that." He knew with the order coming from him, his men wouldn't dare deviate from the plan. "Got that?" he asked, commandingly. He was holding back a spate of coughing, manfully swallowing the built-up phlegm.

"Yes, sir," the man said, and the younger man looked curiously at Alice, wondering who she was to command them or ask the old man for a favor. It was quite an ask.

Alice saw the young man eyeing her and stared him down, making him extremely uncomfortable. He turned his attention back to the old man.

"You don't deviate or improvise unless necessary. If I must repeat any of that, there will be hell to pay!" he threatened, again swallowing against the need to cough and ruin the ominous feel of his commands. "Four of your best, and they better look the part. *No weapons*," he stressed, knowing the man would get the implications.

"Got it," the man promised, giving a little bow and backing from the room until the two of them were alone again.

"Alice, I'll say goodbye for now," he hinted broadly, hoping to hold back the coughing spate that was due.

"Are you sure I can't take care of something for you?" Her head tilted back towards the door where they both knew the hospice nurse would soon be coming through.

"After I'm gone, do what you will. For now, she relieves *some* of the pain. I'd have played with her if I was younger."

"And made her pay," Alice added with a grin. She reached out to the frail man's equally frail hand and clasped it for a moment. "I'm sorry, my friend. See you in the next life?"

"I'll reserve a mansion for you and yours," he promised with a grin. A tear was forming in his eye. He was feeling emotional and not from his medications. He would never see the likes of an Alice Weaver again. He wouldn't want to, but she was something special. He missed the added curves. Her body was a lot different now, but he also liked the punk rock look.

Alice walked out of the room, shutting the door behind her carefully and leaning against it for a moment. Out of the corner of her eye, Alice saw movement down the hall and pretended she didn't see Sandi as she deliberately turned the other way and headed for the stairs. This time, she didn't bother with a window but walked boldly out the front door and down the steps. The man Sebastian had commanded was standing there with the sports track-suited guy, staring curiously and intimidatingly. As she walked out the front door, several guards looked at her curiously as she walked down the drive, obviously having been made aware of her presence inside the mansion. She needed to release some of her nervous energy. She wanted to jog and use the suit she was wearing, but she knew they would think that a sign of fear. She passed through the gate, which magically opened as she approached it, proving she was being watched by the many cameras.

She made her way around the block and back to the Porsche, lamenting the fact that some of the old friends she had made over the years were passing. Sebastian wouldn't be the first or the last. Still, it was like passing a torch. She sighed. Her body wasn't what it once was either. The time in Kazakhstan had really taken a toll. Then she thought about how old she was and shrugged, there was nothing she could do about getting older.

Unbeknownst to Alice, Sebastian had one more conversation after she left and before the pills Sandi supplied him came into effect. He could feel the taste in his mouth that told him he would be drifting soon. The triumph in Sandi's eyes as she administered the liquid meds through the tube in his arm told its own tales. She reluctantly left the room as the man Sebastian had commanded came into the room.

"Artum close the door," Sebastian rasped, waving Sandi away.

Artum waited until Sandi started down the hallway and then stuck his head out to make sure she was gone. He could see her curiosity and knew it was unhealthy. If what he thought was really happening, he would kill her, but someone had asked a favor, and Sebastian had employed the nurse. Artum didn't trust her for some reason. It was in his nature not to trust strangers, regardless of their associates or nationality. Closing the door, he turned back to Sebastian. He was sad to see his uncle looking so frail. He'd always been a man to look up to, but now, he was a shadow of his former self. "Yes, Uncle?" he asked, prompting him. He could see he was going to fall asleep soon.

"No one is to ever touch Alice Weaver and her family. Is that understood?"

"Yes, Uncle, I'll pass the word. Is she one of us?" he asked, wondering at her connection to this Russian-American mobster.

"No, she's outside the system. She's a system to herself. If anyone makes that mistake, there will be hell to pay, and she's died more than once." He started coughing, alarmed that there was blood on the tissue this time. That couldn't be good.

Artum thought perhaps his uncle was exaggerating. How did someone die more than once? "No one touches the Weaver family. I understand."

His uncle grasped his hand, his grip amazingly strong for a moment as he tried to make himself understood. "Artum I'm serious. She will destroy everything I ever built if she feels we betrayed her. She has resources we could only dream of and wouldn't hesitate to take us out. Every...one...of...us." He was fading, and he knew it, but he had to get his point across. There was fear in his voice that Artum dismissed as the ramblings of an old man. Still, she had taken down one of their men and broken his arm, and she was an interesting-looking woman. He could bet she was hot in her younger days.

"I'll keep that in mind, Uncle."

Sebastian began to mumble, trying to tell his great-nephew what Alice had been like twenty years ago, but the drugs were too powerful and too insidious, and he stopped midway through his speech, dozing off. Artum watched to be sure the old man was asleep before he tucked him in respectfully and left him.

* * * * *

"Mrs. Weaver?" a voice woke Alice from her daydream. She glanced at the woman standing before her, her body tensing as though ready to spring up. The woman saw the narrowing of the eyes and was

momentarily startled at their color…were they orange? "I'm sorry. Did I startle you?" the woman asked ingenuously.

"Yes, I'm sorry," she excused herself, having not heard the woman approach. That wasn't like her. Thinking again about Sebastian, she had lost herself in memories. Maybe she was getting old. Still, she had taken that bodyguard down and broken his arm. Those were not the actions of someone who was old. The man had been young and virile, and surprise had been on her side. Secretly, she was proud of herself, even if her body said, *"You're stiffening up from that."* She'd eased the stiffness on the flight back with a little alcohol, something she hadn't indulged in much in her life. That was last night, and now, she had to deal with whatever was before her.

"If you'll come this way, please?" the woman said kindly, indicating that Alice should follow her across the large atrium. The security guards were still surreptitiously watching her, just in case.

She got up, still a little stiff from the activities of a couple days before. She'd slept well the previous night in the hotel, but she was still tired. As they passed security, the woman held out a hand and was given a guest pass. She handed the pass to Alice before the small, blonde woman went through the metal detector. For once, Alice was glad she had left her special, metal belt back in the hotel room with her other clothes. Alice followed the woman into the elevator where she pressed five, and the car rapidly rose. Alice was escorted to a room, not an interrogation room as she'd thought, but to what looked like an office. She didn't miss the one-way mirror. That must be standard issue. She didn't sit down right away. Instead, she looked out the window at the Virginia countryside. Whoever occupied this office enjoyed a nice view.

"Someone will be with you momentarily," the woman informed her as she indicated the seats across from a bare wooden desk.

Alice wondered at the treatment she was receiving. Why wasn't she in an interrogation room? What was the purpose of this? She saw several things she could use to defend herself if necessary, including bookshelves made of wood, scissors, and even a ruler. Was this really someone's office?

"Ms. Weaver?" a voice interrupted her perusal of the relatively bare room and the view outside the window. Alice turned to the man standing in the doorway, who smiled and indicated a seat as he came into the room. "You were asking for Madelyn Korbel?"

She nodded, not saying anything as she sat down.

"She's retired."

"I heard."

He waited, hoping she would say more. When she didn't, he asked, "You have information about Kazakhstan and arms shipments?"

She nodded and waited, examining him as he had her.

He was surprised how close her scrutiny of him was. He had been trained to look for signs from people he interviewed, watching for things that would give away whether they were lying. She didn't give off any of these signs. She just waited. It was almost…predatory.

"Who are you?" Alice asked, tired of waiting.

"I'm sorry. I'm Albert Miller. I worked with Madelyn when she was here."

"Did she retire voluntarily?"

He smiled slightly. She obviously had known Madelyn and her work ethics well. Madelyn had been obsessed with the job and had risen quite high in its ranks…for a woman. The intel she had collected had been very

beneficial to her career. "I'm not at liberty to give out that information. Can you tell me how you knew her?"

"By now, my file should have been pulled, and you will see I supplied her with information from time to time. I now have information that I wish to trade." She folded her arms across her chest, leaned back in the chair with her legs out before her, and looked absolutely relaxed. He wasn't fooled. She was not relaxed in the least. He was quite sure she could spring up and defend herself if needed. He had read some of her file although there wasn't enough time to read it all. Plenty of it had been redacted, and he wondered at that. Who was Alice Weaver that she could uncover information that someone like Madelyn would have used?

"I've read some of your file," he admitted. "Quite a lot has been redacted."

She nodded to acknowledge that but didn't offer an explanation or additional information.

"About Kazakhstan?" he prompted, wondering if this was a dead end, and she was here for some sort of glory. From the little he'd read, he doubted an online trader and investment broker, would have much information that was helpful for the country. He had read the newspaper articles about her disappearance, death, and reappearance. She had claimed she'd been kidnapped, but nothing in their system supported that information. He wondered at that. Authorities should have interviewed her and pursued that lead.

"Nuh uh. I'll give you the information when I'm assured that my family and I will no longer be the victims of the IRS and police witch hunts. When we have an agreement in writing to that effect, I'll give you enough information that the trail to the billions exchanging hands will keep quite a few of you spooks busy for a long time."

He blinked, surprised at her statement. Surely, she was kidding. "I can't make the IRS or the police stop investigating...."

"Yes, you can," she said simply and stopped talking, waiting.

"Ms. Weaver surely you can't think you can walk in here and make demands like that–" he began officiously.

Alice knew she was being jerked around, and it pissed her off. She interrupted him, waving off whatever he had been about to say, "Look, you have a limited window of opportunity to gain my cooperation. Had you really read my entire file, you would know I don't jerk people around, and I don't appreciate having my time wasted. There is a time limit here–"

"Are you threatening me?"

Alice smiled slightly. "Yes, I am, and don't interrupt me again. In fact, I think you should consult Madelyn to see if I'm kidding. There is a short time limit before this information goes public...worldwide."

He blinked again, wondering if she was bluffing and not appreciating the threat. But he could sense she wasn't kidding. His glance took in the mirror at the end of the room, and that simple act alone gave him away.

"I'll wait here if you want to consult with someone in a position of authority, but the clock is ticking. I've set it up so this information will go public shortly. I'd rather give it to you all in exchange for a dismissal of all charges against me and mine."

"If you are guilty of tax fraud–" he began, getting angry, but Alice cut him off.

"You've interrupted me again!" she said, interrupting him. "I am telling you about the time limit, so you don't make the mistake of thinking I won't follow through. I assure you, I don't play those games, and I don't have to bluff. Read my file again. Oh, and you just gave yourself away there," she informed him helpfully. "If you knew nothing about the

- 28 -

charges being brought against me and my estate, then you wouldn't have mentioned tax fraud." Pointing that out gave her immense satisfaction, but it proved they had looked her up and were gathering information. "Run along and get this sorted," she said to him as though talking to a child. "Find someone in a position of authority." When he made no move to get up and do as she told him, she turned away, looked right into the mirror, and grinned. Her smile looked great with the new teeth. "I'm not kidding," she informed the mirror before getting up, putting her hands into the pockets of her pants suit, and looking out at the view again.

"Ms. Weaver, Alice…" he began heatedly, annoyed that she was turning this interview into a travesty. "You can't come in and threaten the CIA."

Alice whirled, amazingly gracefully but so fast it surprised him into silence. "I did not give you permission to call me by my first name, *Mr.* Miller. Learn the courtesies, and you'll go a lot further. Even Psychology 101 classes teach that." She turned back to look out the window and spoke to it, knowing the man was still trying to outwait her. "If you are thinking you can hold me indefinitely, you are right. Only a couple people know where I am, but they are going to blow the whistle if I don't make an appearance or contact them in a period of time. You are wasting my time, Mr. Miller." She went silent, and the questions he tried to fire at her were not answered as she stood there, looking out. Alice Weaver had the patience, and the eyes, of a cat.

He finally looked exasperatedly at the mirror, rose, and left the office. Alice heard the lock engage and laughed. It wouldn't matter if they locked her into a jail cell. Nothing could be worse than what she had gone through in Central America, Russia, or Kazakhstan.

It took another half hour before a woman came in to try using the same tactics and the same questions, and Alice stopped repeating herself. "That's it! Contact Madelyn Korbel, or we're done!"

"Ms. Weaver, I assure you we can detain you and your family for–"

That was when Alice unleashed some of her inner self. She leaned across the desk and breathed into the woman's face, "Touch my family, and I'll make sure the people who have this information make fools of the CIA, the FBI, and even the Secret Service. This will embarrass many powerful politicians in this country and several other countries. What do you think will happen to *your* job…*all* your jobs, if that happens?"

"What is the information you have that you think will affect us all so greatly?" she asked, but Alice was done. They had threatened her family, as she had known they would. She wouldn't speak to them again unless they brought her Madelyn, and she told them so.

They left her waiting for two days in that office without food and water, and she ended up squatting in a corner and peeing because she had no facilities either. Their wood floor was no longer pristine. She made no move to break up the room, either sitting angled in the chair, so the mirror had her back or laying on the desk as she dozed. Already sleep-deprived, she knew what they were doing. She could handle it, and this office was more comfortable than some of the cells she had been in. She was disgusted by the lack of facilities and almost wished for a jail cell, so she could use the toilet. Her own fastidious nature didn't appreciate the situation in the least.

* * * *

The cars turned one by one into the long drive in the Connecticut countryside, perfectly in sync. They were like puppets on a string, all of them black with blackened windows. Madelyn saw them before they stopped before her circular drive. Only feds traveled in packs like that, so she wasn't surprised to see Clifford Wolf step from one of the black Suburbans. She met him at the front door, saying sardonically before he could open his mouth, "Whatever it is, no. I'm retired."

Cliff laughed, knowing she wouldn't have answered a mere phone call, but they needed her. The file on Alice Weaver had frightened a few people who knew more than they admitted as they read through portions of it. The woman had been instrumental in several things they weren't allowed to discuss without the proper clearance. If Ms. Weaver had information on arms shipments, and her threats indicated she did, they needed Madelyn to at least clue them in on how to deal with her. They were one step away from imprisoning Alice and her family, if necessary. Some of the gist of what they had been able to get out of her had been verified, and they needed the details.

"Don't even try the *'let's be friends'* tactic, Director Kolby. I'm serious. I'm retired!" She went to close her door, but he grabbed it.

"What about national security?" he began, but she waved her hand dismissively.

"I've given my life for the CIA. Don't start that crap," she said angrily.

"What if we give–?"

"No matter what you give me, it isn't enough. I've given my all, and I'm retired, dammit!"

"Alice Weaver," he said, watching her closely and seeing her blanch. "What do you know of her?"

"Did you arrest her?" she gasped out, looking genuinely frightened. Her hand came up to the top of her blouse, worrying the fabric there as she waited for his answer.

"No, she came in voluntarily. She's asking for a deal." He watched her curiously, wondering why that name had caused such an extreme reaction in this normally unperturbable woman.

"She came in voluntarily? She's where? Langley?" She sounded incredulous.

He nodded. "She walked in of her own accord two days ago. We're holding her for information."

"You haven't escalated your interrogation tactics, have you?"

"You think we should?"

She immediately shook her head. "No, I wouldn't suggest that at all."

"May I come in?" he asked, growing weary of standing on her doorstep.

Madelyn made a gesture. It wasn't really a welcome, but it certainly indicated he could come in. She saw the others standing by the vehicles and looking about. That was going to make an impression with her neighbors, if they could see the men and women in black suits wearing sunglasses. If that didn't scream CIA or some other secret service, she didn't know what did. She sighed at the inconvenience. She was *retired*, dammit!

* * * * *

"Ms. Weaver, I'm sure we can make a deal," Mr. Miller tried interrogating her again, telling her these things as another woman, a cleaning lady from the look of her, cleaned up the corner Alice had

squatted in. "If you do not cooperate, you must realize we can't help you with the tax lien. The IRS will forfeit your bank accounts, the insurance policies, all your real estate, as well as your children's trust funds."

Alice didn't react. She knew they were finally doing their homework on her. His stating all these things made it more obvious to her that they believed her when she said she had information regarding the arms shipments.

"The IRS is alleging that you defrauded the government of tens of millions of dollars that you didn't pay taxes on. We can't offer you a deal unless you tell us more. And part of making that up will clearly be you handing over your ill-gotten gains. Tell us the things you did to attain those monies and the real estate involved."

Alice nearly smiled; she had anticipated this. It was why she had exchanged cash for the real estate that Sasha now owned outright. She didn't want her name on any of it. The government of the United States, much less Russia, would never find the monies. She glanced at the woman finishing up in the corner, who had stiffened at the man's words, unconsciously acknowledging that she was listening. Alice didn't believe she was a cleaning woman and wondered who she was.

"You paid, what, ten million for your Palos Altos' property? I bet it's worth a whole helluva lot more all these years later," he commented.

Alice finally looked at him in a bored fashion, but he swallowed as he realized her odd eyes weren't the shade of yellow he had become accustomed to. They were listed as brown in her file, but right now, they were decidedly orange. "Are you going to produce Madelyn Korbel or not?" she asked, her voice also sounding bored.

"You've been informed that Madelyn Korbel has retired," he told her, trying to imply with his tone of voice that she wasn't too bright.

"But she's not dead," Alice said in a murmur and turned to look out the window again.

He tried to go back to his agenda of intimidating her. "The analysis of your assets, the sum the IRS expects to recover, nearly covers the estimated costs of the investigation to date."

Alice laughed. It was a genuine laugh, and this puzzled him. He couldn't figure her out. He glanced at the mirror and shrugged slightly. He didn't know how to interrogate such a witness. She could sense that they had ascertained she wasn't intimidated, and she hadn't given them anything really, and then….

"Vashti Baltizar, Leonid Baltizar, Alexander or Xander Baltizar, the Bogomolov family, Filipov, Kozlov," she chanted, ticking off the names that were indelibly inscribed in her mind. She would remember them forever.

"Who are these people?" he asked.

Alice turned her orange eyes on the idiot interrogator. "You really are a novice at this, aren't you? Why are you the one chosen to talk to me? You don't know how to do this," she gestured across the table, indicating the ill-fated interrogation. "I give you the names of some of the most notorious mobsters on the planet and you ask me who they are. They really scraped the barrel with you and your skills, didn't they? Let me guess…last in your class?" She smiled slightly, enjoying the fact that she was making him squirm. And, he *was* squirming, a sure sign her questions and statements were making him uncomfortable.

"Furthermore, the IRS hasn't gone through due process. Do you know what the term due process means?" she asked him as though he were a child, and she had to explain things to him. She was using his own tone of voice from earlier against him, taking delight in humiliating him. "Due

process refers to the general principal that the United States government can't take away a person's rights or property without a legal proceeding. I haven't been given due process. Instead, someone's vendetta is getting the best of them, and they are using the IRS as a punitive measure. I just gave you the names of mobsters that I will give the CIA further information on. In exchange, I want a clean slate. I want the investigations by the IRS and police stopped, and I want this vendetta stopped," she gestured again, "and I want you to give me the names of those who instigated this vendetta!." She stopped, staring him in the eyes as he squirmed further, before she swung to the mirror, staring through it at the people behind its reflection, or so they felt, before turning and looking out the window again. She wouldn't say anything further.

This silence, which was stretching out to days, and their further investigations into Alice Weaver, as well as the names she had given them, had them scurrying to find out where Madelyn Korbel lived.

* * * * *

"Director Kolby I am not at liberty to tell you anything about Alice Weaver other than what you can find in her files," she gestured to the thick files of mostly redacted information that he had pulled from his briefcase. She nearly laughed as one file, at least four-inches thick and heavy, flipped open and nearly every other line was blacked out.

"I am the director of the CIA. I can assure you I have clearance," he chuckled, sitting back and waiting, glancing around the comfortable and sophisticated living room they were sitting in. The furniture was as elegant as the woman before him. "Who is Alice Weaver, and why haven't I heard about her before?"

Madelyn fidgeted slightly, wondering if she should even say anything. She could refuse. She wasn't in that game anymore. Politics had forced her out, but she had been surprised to learn how relieved she was to be out of the spy game. The information in her head alone was invaluable. She glanced at the files, nearly laughing at how little information on Alice Weaver was contained there. "You could subpoena the original records."

"Apparently, there is no *time*," he said exasperatedly, sighing loudly.

"Why don't you tell me what you do know?" she asked instead of volunteering anything.

"Why don't you tell me what you know?" he countered, wondering why she was so reluctant to assist on this.

Madelyn smiled but shook her head. She gestured at the files. "You have what you need there."

"Alice Weaver is requesting that you interview her."

Madelyn's heart leapt into her throat, nearly choking her as she shook her head. "I'm retired," she repeated.

"I've heard that somewhere," he smiled, showing he wasn't about to let her off the hook so easily. "She's named a number of Russian mobsters, oligarchs some call them."

"And?" she asked, intrigued despite herself. How had Alice Weaver gotten involved with Russian oligarchs?

"All dead. Some by mysterious circumstances. The whole family in some situations. The pictures we were able to obtain are rather gruesome."

She blanched at this news and then quipped, "Well, isn't that law enforcement's problem then?"

"What is the connection? Why would Alice Weaver know these people, and who is she?" He gestured at the file. "What would a stockbroker or a day trader know of these people?"

"You'll have to ask her."

"Believe me, we've tried."

"Man or woman?"

"Huh?"

"Did you send a man or a woman to interrogate her?"

"A man. Why? Would she respond better to a woman?"

"Did he insult her? Was he condescending in any way?"

He laughed. Madelyn obviously knew this Alice Weaver well. "She called him a novice. She accused him of being last in his class."

Madelyn sat back on her couch, laughing despite herself. "Then there you have it. You won't get anything else from her. She's the most...stubborn individual," she understated, "I have ever had the misfortune to come across."

"What exactly was your relationship with her?"

"Exactly that," she indicated the file. Her eyes gave nothing away as she stared directly into his. "Occasionally, she had information we could use."

"And how did this come about...occasionally? Files this thick didn't come about with random interrogations or information."

"It's all there, if you care to read," she hedged, but it was a weak hedge, and they both knew it.

"Why don't you come back and interview her?" he asked.

"What makes you think I would come back after all this. I'm *retired*," she reiterated meaningfully.

"We both know you got the shaft on that, and you'd have had my job if the administration wasn't what it is. Politics are the bane of our existence, and it sucks."

"What makes you think Alice Weaver has anything you can use?" she asked, wondering what they had gotten out of her other than Russian oligarchs. What had Alice dangled before them? What shiny lure was she using to catch them?

"There are...*rumors*," he said, hedging himself, "that the media may have gotten hold of some rather embarrassing information. We need to confirm, but they are being amazingly tight-lipped about the information and their sources, citing the First Amendment. Alice mentioned arms shipments in Kazakhstan and Russia."

Madelyn's eyes suddenly became so focused it was alarming. Her slate gray eyes were sharp, and she was listening intently. "Will I be put back on the payroll at the same grade and clearance?" she asked suddenly.

Surprised at the sudden change, he looked at her in alarm. Which part of that had triggered her? "When exactly did you change your mind?"

"If Alice Weaver says she has information on arms shipments in Kazakhstan and Russia, you can bet she has something to back that up. I want my same clearance, so I can cut a deal with her, and we can get this information before the media releases it. I assure you, the panic that would ensue wouldn't be worth our jobs."

"Tell me," he ordered, but she shook her head.

"This was on a "need to know," Director Wolf, and you really don't want to know," she assured him. "I am not authorized to ever release this information. Do what you have to do," she said, gesturing to his phone and getting up from the couch. "I'll go pack."

He sat there a moment before he reached for his phone. Whatever Madelyn Korbel knew, he wanted to know too. Whatever or whoever Alice Weaver was, he wanted answers.

Langley was the name of the McLean neighborhood where the CIA was located. Supposedly, the Central Intelligence Agency was a civilian foreign intelligence service of the United States' federal government. Tasked with gathering, processing, and analyzing national security information from around the world, too often politicians and world leaders mistook its mandate as something they could use for their own benefit and not for the United States. As one of the principal members of the U.S. Intelligence Community, which included the Federal Bureau of Investigation (FBI), they reported to the Director of National Intelligence. This information was then passed through those offices to the president and the cabinet, so they could make informed decisions regarding both foreign and domestic policy.

Unlike the FBI, which was supposed to be a domestic security service, the CIA has no law enforcement function. Their only mandate is to gather overseas intelligence and limited domestic intelligence. They are also the only agency in the intelligence community authorized to carry out covert action at the behest of the president. If Alice Weaver, a civilian, had the information she implied, the CIA should know about it, so they could act on it.

With one of the largest budgets of all the Intelligence Community (IC), the CIA was authorized to carry out covert actions and influence foreign politics. The CIA had expanded its role over the years to include covert paramilitary operations, counter-terrorism activities, and cyber operations.

Madelyn looked through the information they had on Alice Weaver, laughing as she filled in the blanks of the blacked out or redacted information on the woman. She knew a lot more than she could ever say.

If Alice Weaver said she had this information, Madelyn, for one, believed her.

She looked at what the IRS had on Alice Weaver: bank and tax fraud for failing to file a foreign bank account under an assumed name, tax evasion, grand larceny, criminal liability, but she realized there weren't enough specifics, which the IRS would need to make these charges stick. The allegations were vaguely worded, and Madelyn knew the agency was coming down hard on the citizen in the hope she would fold and implicate herself. They didn't know Alice Weaver.

In 1970, the Racketeer Influenced and Corrupt Organizations Act (RICO) federal law was enacted to combat organized crime in the United States. It allowed prosecution and civil penalties for racketeering activities. She could see what the IRS was trying to build here against Alice, but she could also see from the tax forms Alice had filed that most of the money was legitimate. It was only after Alice had been reported dead that someone, a Portia Spiros and an Andie Wilson, had found additional information and filed the appropriate paperwork. The IRS had seized on that instead of just imposing taxes and penalties for the 'oversight.' Nothing Alice had done, and nothing indicated here, was a RICO violation. There was no racketeering and nothing criminal, but the IRS was trying to make a case of it and prove there was. Why? Madelyn looked up from her seat in the SUV transporting her. She was going through all the current paperwork, so she would be up to snuff before she saw Alice Weaver once again after all these years.

As she started in on the police investigation, she was disappointed to find opinions and speculation but few hard facts. Someone had a bee in their bonnet from what she could see. They had gone to Alice's home and initiated a hell of a search. The yard had been dug up in the last few days.

They were looking for money that was supposedly buried in her yard. They were also looking for a safe, and they found two in her office. They were able to open one safe, and the other had been opened by the homeowner, Kathy Weaver. So, Alice had married. That was interesting. It also made Alice vulnerable. She saw where the interrogator had threatened Alice, not very bright on the interrogator's part, and her response was that he had made an enemy for life.

She read the transcript of a phone conversation as she listened to the recording they had given her, since Alice Weaver's phones were now tapped.

"Mrs. Weaver, we'd like you to come down to the police department for an interview," the voice on the phone informed her.

"I never applied for a position in your department," Alice responded blandly. Madelyn nearly laughed at the dry reply. She also knew that going to a police department without her lawyer would be foolish. They would question her, and anything she said could and would be used against her in a court of law. Alice wouldn't make this easy for them, not if she could help it. Alice was far too smart to fall for their ploy.

"Do you find this amusing?"

"No. Do you?" Alice played with her prey a little more before she let them off the hook. "If you have any further questions, you will have to talk to my lawyer."

"Which one?"

Alice laughed into the phone before she hung up, and Madelyn smiled. That woman wasn't going to fall for anything.

She looked curiously at the inventory of the house, a joint effort of the IRS and the police at this point. She knew that would piss off any homeowner. Strangely, they were allowing Kathy and their children to

stay in the house. Children? Hmmm, another vulnerability on Alice's part. Very interesting. She wondered if this wife of Alice's knew where she was.

* * * * *

Kathy didn't know where Alice was, and this, more than anything else over the past few days, pissed her off. Alice had left a note that Kathy was certain she wasn't expected to find right away, but the police and the IRS, who had obtained a federal search warrant, had leapt upon it immediately.

"Where has your wife gone?"

"Did she know this warrant was coming?"

"Has she left you to face this alone?

The questions came fast and furious. They were all accusatory, and Kathy simply didn't know the answers. Everything was making her question Alice and her intentions since she had been left out of the loop once again. Fortunately, after being married to Alice all these years, she was smart enough to know not to respond to the many questions.

The backhoes and front-end loaders that dug up the landscaping and the lawns were frightening, and they made a general mess of the yard, but it was the officers going through the house that managed to completely unnerve Kathy. She had been tempted to just let them find the safe with the bear trap on their own. As it was, it was a near thing because when she disclosed its location, they wanted the combination to get into it. She asked that she be allowed to disarm it first. Seeing the look on the officers' and agents' faces when they realized that someone's hand or arm would have been impaled on the spikes of the trap gave her a note of satisfaction. She could see that the children, who she wouldn't let out of

her sight with all these intimidating strangers in her home, were shocked about the second safe as well. The whole family had known about the wall safe, but only Alice and Kathy and a few now dead individuals knew about the floor safe.

They found the hidden panel in the master bedroom, but Alice must have foreseen that possibility and emptied it. Kathy was relieved since it had contained cash money that she couldn't readily explain as well as various passports in different names. When the authorities found their real passports, they were confiscated.

The meticulous inventory of all the items in the house took forever, and Kathy was losing her patience as she helplessly watched the officers going through their things. They were prying boards off the floor and walls looking for more hidden devices, and they were pulling apart the furniture, turning everything upside down, looking for hidden pockets and going through everyone's dresser drawers, clothes, and personal effects. They were also trying to question the children which Kathy wouldn't allow. Finally, a phone call came in that stopped all their searching. Whoever was on the other end of the phone had Mr. Smith standing at attention. He was trying to argue but ultimately conceded.

"That's it. Let's go!" he said to the men and women staring at him. "We're done here...*for now*," he added ominously, glaring at Kathy accusatorily.

Slowly, everyone filed out of the Palos Verdes house, tracking dirt on its beautiful floors as they left. No one apologized. Few, if any, looked contrite. Kathy looked out to make sure they had all left and saw some of the neighbors gathered at the end of the driveway. They were looking on and discussing what was going on behind the wide-open gates. She saw the Pasternack family and Em's little friend, Carmen, staring before she

closed the door to their curious looks. Kathy was left there, her children in her arms, although Sean was angry enough for all of them.

"Why did they behave that way, Mom?" Emily asked, sounding frightened.

"I don't know, honey. I don't know," Kathy answered, watching as the many cars, the heavy-duty equipment, and the SUVs left the property. It was a mess, and it would cost tens of thousands of dollars to get the lawns and landscaping back in order.

"Do you think Mom knows?" Sean asked, sounding belligerent. He had been ready to fight the agents and the police for access to his room. Kathy had gotten him away but not before a few of his insults had landed home, and as a result, his room had been tossed a little more frantically than the others.

"I don't know," Kathy admitted, angry that Alice wasn't here to witness this. She knew the final humiliation would come when they ordered her to leave their home with her children. She jumped a foot when the doorbell rang.

"They're back!" Emily squawked, sounding frightened.

"They wouldn't have rung the doorbell, stupid," Sean said, still sounding angry.

"Sean!" Kathy's tone warning him about calling his sister names. It was something she had always discouraged her children from doing, but without Alice here to back her up, it was sometimes hard, especially with teenagers. She pulled him back from the door, going to answer it herself.

"Yes?" she said to the men standing there intimidatingly. She looked between the dark-haired men, wondering who and what they were. They were dressed in leather coats and had a distinctive aura about them. They looked dangerous from what she could see.

"Mrs. Weaver?" the man in front asked, trying to soften his facial expression and be courteous. "Ms. Alice asked that I stop by."

"Alice?" she asked, confused. Alice's note had said she had gone to stop this madness. Apparently, she had been mistaken as she glanced past the men at the destruction to their yard. There were piles of sod and dirt, and flowers were strewn haphazardly where they had dug up the entire lawn and gardens.

"Yes, I'm Sebastian's nephew, Artum. He and Alice spoke the other day and arranged that I stop by. I didn't think it prudent to butt in while the agents were here," he told her, trying to sound kind.

"Alice arranged…?" she asked, confused. It was obvious they had seen the ransacking of her yard and home.

"Yes, ma'am. Is there somewhere we can talk privately?" he asked, glancing at the teenagers looking on.

"Um, yeah, I guess," she said, holding the door wide and stepping aside, so the two men could enter. She glanced at the teens, who were staring wide-eyed. Sean looked belligerent. "You two start cleaning up your rooms."

"We didn't make the mess," Sean pointed out.

"I know, but you will feel better when things are straightened out. I don't think those officers are going to come back and clean it up for you, so please get started."

Sean looked like he was going to argue but after looking at their guests and then back at his mother, he shrugged angrily and stomped up the stairs.

Emily stared at the men for a moment before she left without a word but glanced back repeatedly, gauging how frightened her mom was. She didn't know why Alice had left them alone to handle all this, but she was

certain it was for their own good. What Alice could have done, she didn't know, but she had the utmost faith in her mom.

"I'd ask you to sit down," Kathy gestured to the living room where the cushions were all off the furniture and there was a tear in the couch, which had cost them well over five grand. That couch had survived the children growing up and a dog, yet the officers had felt obliged to tear it open. "But as you can see…" she left off, gesturing helplessly and feeling embarrassed. "You said Sebastian sent you?"

"Yes, Alice came to see him, and they worked out an arrangement. I am to take you to our plane, which is standing by, and get you out of the country."

Kathy was stunned. Alice thought things were bad enough that they should leave the country?

"I was to come get you if the IRS or the police were about to pounce, but I had some bad information about that," he said, glancing at the other man, who was looking about and had the good grace to blush at this statement.

"Wait! You and Alice knew that they might do this?"

"Yes, ma'am," he said, wanting to just put her in their car and take off, so he could get her to the plane that was ready and waiting for her.

"Where is Alice?" she asked, suddenly wary of going with anyone she didn't know.

"I don't know," he admitted, glancing up the stairs where he could see the teenagers were listening. He nearly smiled, knowing it was something he would have done if he had been in their shoes.

"Well, I'm not going. I'm not leaving my home and my children's home. I don't know what Alice was thinking. If we leave, we look guilty!" she said, outraged.

"I don't know about that, ma'am," he said respectfully. "All I know is I was instructed to get you out before they did this, and I failed. I have a plane standing by to take you to South America, and Ms. Alice stated you would know where to go from there. I have cash for you to live on–" he began, but Kathy silenced him with a raised hand.

"I don't know you. I don't know Sebastian. Apparently, I don't really know my wife," she answered, sounding tired and angry. "I won't be going anywhere, so you can save your breath."

"I was to get you out," he began, reverting to his old ways when someone didn't obey his commands. "We were to get you out," he said ominously.

"What are you going to do? Pick me up physically and haul me out of my own home?" she asked, trying not to sound nervous.

"I was told…" he began, but Sean appeared just then, carrying an aluminum baseball bat.

"You gentlemen had better leave," he said, holding the bat up in a way that showed he could easily bring it into play.

The man with Artum made a move as though to grab something out of his waistband.

"If you move any farther, I'm going to bash in your head or break your arm," Sean said conversationally, trying to sound like one of his heroes on TV. Inside his heart was beating hard.

"Yeah, and I'll shove this up your dick," Emily said crudely, coming up behind Sean with a wooden baseball bat.

"Emily!" Kathy castigated her, sounding horrified. "Give me that," she said, wrenching the bat out of her daughter's hands. She looked up at the amused Artum. "I think you and your associate had better leave. Apparently, we aren't going anywhere."

He nodded tightly, knowing Sebastian would be furious. Alice hadn't said what to do if her wife refused to leave. He wanted to just rush the helpless woman and her children, sure they could overwhelm them, but he was amused that they would try to defend themselves with baseball bats. He eyed Kathy. Maybe she wasn't as helpless as she appeared. "I will check back in case you change your mind," he said respectfully, nodding coldly to the young man and smiling charmingly at the skinny girl. The man with him followed resentfully behind, glaring at the teens.

"Did you see that house? Even tossed there are some nice things," he said as they got in the Cadillac.

"Sebastian said they weren't to be touched. Keep your greedy eyes off them," Artum warned, wondering what he was going to report to Sebastian. He only hoped Sebastian would be asleep when he got back to the safe house.

* * * * *

Alice was hungry. It had been three days, and they hadn't fed her. Her belligerent peeing in their corner had finally forced them to produce a bucket she could use but nothing better. At least, they could have put her in an office or an interrogation room that had a toilet, but then, they wouldn't have the benefit of the two-way mirror.

Alice had the fortitude to outwait them. She'd been hungry before, and she'd been interrogated before, and she wasn't about to budge. She was, however, wondering if some of the safeguards she had put in place were failing at this point or what was going on. She wished she knew, and these morons they had sent to interrogate her weren't giving away much.

"You realize that lying to the CIA is a crime?" the current one asked.

"Yes, and so is lying to the FBI," she returned agreeably, amusing herself as she surprised them both by answering. Her silence had been *unnerving* to those who had tried to question her.

"How did you get the information on these men?" he tried again, indicating the names she had given them.

"What men?" she returned, sounding innocent and infuriating those less inclined to play the games they were playing.

"The names you gave us!"

"What names?" she asked.

"Would it help if I played back the tape?"

"That would only prove that I am being taped. Did I consent to being taped? Isn't it a crime to tape someone without their consent or knowledge? It's a crime in many states not to have it posted," she pointed out, looking around as though searching for such a post, which they both knew was preposterous.

They tried tag-teaming her, proving they had delved further into her FBI, CIA, and possibly police-related files. "So, what are you, some kind of hacker or something?"

Alice's lips moved into a semblance of a smile as she turned to face her accuser. "Yeah, okay. We will go with that."

The less-experienced interrogators allowed themselves to be overheard. Alice knew they sometimes did that on purpose, but as her patience was wearing thin and time was running out, she didn't rise to their bait.

Finally, on the fourth day, the most delicious aroma of steak and potatoes preceded her interrogator into the room. Alice looked up, her head practically snapping to attention as she looked in the eyes of Madelyn Korbel. She smiled, pleased to see the woman and noting the grey hairs that hadn't been there the last time she had seen her so long ago.

"Ms. Korbel it has been a long time," she greeted her, watching as Madelyn put a covered plate in front of her and placed an identical plate at her own seat as she sat down.

"We weren't–" began the young interrogator, gesturing towards the food.

"To feed her?" Madelyn finished for him. "Run along, Johnny," she said, making shooing gestures. "You're in the big leagues now, and it's against the Geneva Convention to withhold basic human necessities. Furthermore, Ms. Weaver is not a prisoner." She smiled at Alice, sharing a glimmer of humor with her as the young man practically ran out of the room to report to his superior. He didn't know who this woman was, but she had been let into the room. Madelyn looked at Alice. "Hungry?" she asked.

"Thirsty," Alice acknowledged, and she watched as Madelyn approached the cart that had rolled the wonderful smelling food into the room. She saw it also contained an ice-cold pitcher of water, and the condensation dripped down the outside as Madelyn poured them both a full glass.

"You don't drink alcohol, if I remember correctly," Madelyn began conversationally.

"Not often, no," Alice admitted as she sipped slowly at the water. She knew drinking too fast would cause her stomach to clench after all these days deprived of water. "Thank you. That hit the spot," she said, saluting the CIA woman with her glass.

"Please, help yourself. I hadn't eaten either, so I had them make us both steak and potatoes," Madelyn told her, gesturing to the covered plates. Alice removed her cover and found they also had onions and

carrots on the plate. She saw the steak was deliciously well done as she cut into it.

"You *remembered*," she stated, flattered.

"I did. Well done because you don't like your cows to moo when you cut into them," Madelyn said, sitting down across from Alice and lifting her own lid. The steak on her plate was only done on the outside. She lifted her silverware, put her napkin across her lap, and then cut into her own steak. "Ketchup?" she offered Alice, taking steak sauce for her own.

"Thank you," Alice answered. They were both quiet while they ate as much as they could. Alice's stomach had shrunk, so she couldn't eat as much as she would have liked, and she wisely stopped when she realized she was full.

"Was it good?" Madelyn asked, seeing how much her guest had left on her plate.

"Delicious," Alice agreed, wiping her lips delicately with the napkin.

"Would you like to take a walk?" Madelyn asked, glancing at the mirror where she knew there were a bevy of agents that had just watched them eat.

Alice was amused. "How do you know I won't run off?"

Madelyn grinned. "I think you have some information you wish to trade?"

"I do," she agreed, nodding.

"Then, I think some exercise is order, so we can walk off this excellent meal and get down to business," she stated, rising and stretching slightly. She was pleased to note that Alice checked her out.

Alice rose too and cracked her neck. She would be pleased to get out of this room and knew without a doubt they would be followed.

Madelyn didn't say anything as she escorted Alice out of the office, to the bank of elevators, down to the lobby, and out the front door. The grounds were extensive, and they walked for a while, enjoying the cool, fresh air of Virginia.

"You know they found your storage unit?"

"They did?" Alice asked, sounding surprised, but with a glimmer of humor in her eyes. She had known they would, but they wouldn't find anything other than her completely outdated computers. All the information she wanted from the computers was gone including the programs and whatever she had found using them. The computers were mere shells of what they had once been.

"Shouldn't you be asking which storage unit?" Madelyn asked, knowing Alice was playing with her.

"Okay…" she hesitated for a moment, "Which one?"

"Do you have more than one?" Madelyn asked.

The humor increased in Alice's sparkling eyes, but the irises were changing. Madelyn thought she saw them turning a shade of orange. That must be a trick of the light, right? Then, remembering a previous experience years ago, she realized that orange wasn't a good sign. She'd prefer Alice Weaver's eyes to remain their normal brown. Even yellow wasn't too bad, but orange was positively dangerous.

"You tell me?" Alice asked patiently, willing to play the game. She cocked her head sideways, waiting for an answer.

"You could do this all day, couldn't you?"

"Do what?" she asked innocently, a ripple of a smile twitching her lips. Her eyes were dancing, and they were most definitely turning yellow.

She didn't know what it was about this woman's eyes that entranced her so. They also made her decidedly uncomfortable, but so long as Alice was smiling....

"What do you want, Alice?" she asked, using her first name since they were alone.

"I want a letter of apology from Mr. Smith on behalf of the IRS. I want all inquiries into my finances to be dropped by the IRS, and I want my funds released. I want the police to stop their inquiry as well, and I want the name of whoever started all these actions."

"You think the CIA can stop an IRS audit?" Madelyn asked, amused. It seemed such a small request for someone of Alice's...*expertise* to come all this way.

"Yes, you can do that...and more. What I offer in exchange is ties to organized crime in Russia."

"You gave us those names," Madelyn mentioned.

"I have more: dates, times, and locations as well," she told the woman.

Madelyn had thought there would be more. Alice was the best poker player out there where lives were concerned. She wouldn't have been here if she merely wanted the IRS inquiries dropped. It wasn't an even exchange, and she wondered how much of that information Alice was really going to give them.

"Okay, you give us–" she began, but Alice was already shaking her head.

"I want the letter of apology from Smith, another from the IRS, and an official letter stating that all these inquiries were a bureaucratic mistake and will be dropped. I want the same assurances from the police. I want *immunity*," she stated.

"Now, you are asking for more–" she began, mentally going over the police report she had read about the woman Alice had nearly killed and yet saved.

"Yes, and I will continue upping the ante as you continue delaying. You see, the media is in possession of all this information. They are just waiting for the password to access the many drives I sent them containing everything I am offering to tell you. Imagine if it were to go public that the CIA was giving guns and other things to the public in Russia, as well as to the mobsters, gangsters, and organized crime. You all are going to have a big, black eye," Alice pointed out matter-of-factly.

"How do I know you really have all that?" Madelyn asked, her training forcing her to hedge in order to buy her some time to think.

Alice had been anticipating that and merely smiled, halting their walk to look up at the taller woman. "When have you ever known me to lie over important things such as this? You know I'm not bluffing."

Madelyn did know, and she knew that if someone in the CIA was directing this, Alice and her family were as good as dead. It had been clever and just like the Alice she knew to hedge her bets with the media. She didn't doubt for a moment that they had such drives in their possession. "So, if I get this letter of apology and the immunity, you will give me the drive?"

"Of course," Alice responded, sounding insulted.

"And the password?" she verified, knowing her simple tricks.

Alice laughed, glancing at the many agents that were following them and almost surrounding them. They didn't realize it, but she could have gotten away despite their numbers. They were very good, but she was better. She also didn't want to have to do that. "Yes, the password too," she agreed with a grin.

Madelyn relaxed slightly. She knew that nothing was at all what it seemed with Alice. She knew this probably wasn't all the woman had for them, but she would take what she could get. "Let's get you comfortable while I see what I can get for you. How much time do I have?"

"Not enough. They wasted a lot of time bringing you in."

"I was *retired*," she told the blonde, reiterating something she had said time and again to various people.

"What? Were you holed up in a cabin deep in the woods somewhere?" Alice teased. They shared a laugh. Neither of them was really the outdoorsy types.

"Let's just say I was reluctant," she told her instead.

"Did you retire, or were you forced out?" Alice asked as they turned back towards the buildings, their followers trying to remain unobtrusive and failing, at least to Alice's sharp eyes.

Madelyn sighed. She too saw their followers. It was like old times. She'd have to talk to a few people about better surveillance techniques. These were sloppy. "Let's just say the latter and leave it at that," she told Alice.

Alice nodded knowingly. She wouldn't ask further. They were too close to the building, and she was certain there were listening devices. She hadn't considered that Madelyn might be wearing a wire and maybe she should have. "Mind letting me use the bathroom?" she asked.

Madelyn sighed again. "Your peeing in that room didn't go over well," she told her as she led her past security, nodding to one of the older guards she recognized who remembered her from back in the day. She headed to a public restroom.

"Then they should have provided better accommodations," Alice told her, starting to feel uncomfortable from the food they had eaten, which

was going right through her. She was relieved to have a toilet and toilet paper available to her, even if it was one ply…the cheap bastards!

Madelyn, who had waited for Alice, had also signaled a couple officers and given instructions to make accommodations available for their guest. Alice was not a prisoner, and she made that clear to them.

As Alice washed her hands a while later, she glanced up to exchange a look in the mirror with Madelyn. The CIA operative glanced down the length of the bathroom and back at Alice, letting her know they were being observed even here. Alice didn't flicker an eyelash to indicate she understood the woman. She dried her hands and followed her out of the bathroom and back towards the bank of elevators. They went to the third floor this time and entered a room with a bed and a full bathroom. Clothes were laid out on the bed.

"Give me a few hours to see what I can get going on our end," Madelyn told her as she showed her the room. "If you need me, they'll let me know," she indicated the guards outside Alice's room.

Alice nodded, pleased there were no two-way mirrors, but she was certain the room was bugged and was determined she wouldn't say anything. She waited for Madelyn to leave the room in order to strip, shower, and change into the rather nice clothing they had supplied her. It even fit, which surprised her. They had confiscated her identification and hotel room key, so she had nothing to transfer from the old clothes. She sat and dozed off on the bed as she waited. She wondered how much time she had left…how much time *they* had left.

* * * * *

"What are you going to offer her?" Director Wolf asked Madelyn when she returned to the office they had given her. She had gone straight to her phone and looked up, startled, as he entered her office without knocking.

Replacing the phone in its cradle, she swallowed her annoyance. "I'm going to give her exactly what she asked for," she responded, and before he could interrupt, she added, "after I verify a couple things."

"How do you know her?" he asked again and was annoyed when she wouldn't answer him. "You do know I'm your supervisor, right?"

"Yes, sir," she said patiently, waiting for him to leave as she glanced pointedly at the phone.

He sighed. Somedays he hated his job. Secrets within secrets; that was the job. He had to trust her. This woman had been a valuable asset, and he had been sorry to lose her to politics a couple years ago. He'd had to pull a few strings to get her reinstated and had been surprised that she would even condescend to come back. Whoever Alice Weaver was, he was grateful that her presence had brought this woman back. He nodded stiffly as he waved and left the office.

Madelyn made several calls, working up the chain of command at the Palos Verdes and Los Angles police stations and getting information that wasn't on the computer yet. She was amused to learn that both departments were experiencing computer malfunctions that had spread to Pasadena and several other stations including the FBI but had been stopped at their firewall. Later, she discovered the FBI was experiencing their own version of the virus. It was slowly spreading through their system, which didn't really have outside access. Something or someone from within had to have planted it. She thought about that as she was on hold with the powers that be at the IRS, getting information she would

need in order to proceed with Alice Weaver. She glanced at her computer and saw their *guest* was sleeping on the bed in her room.

* * * * *

"Do you really think what this civilian has to offer is of such great value that we can simply dismiss the charges the IRS has on her, much less disregard what the police suspect?" she was challenged by one of the agents in the meeting she attended later that day.

"Yes, I do. I've checked with my media contacts, and it is confirmed that a drive was delivered to each of their stations, and they are awaiting the key code to open it and retrieve the promised information. I don't know that the drive is from Ms. Weaver, but if she says she has information that will be embarrassing for us if we don't comply, I believe her."

"You realize this is blackmail?" one of the men pointed out, sounding angry.

"Yes, it is, and we deal with that every day of the week," Madelyn countered. "Think of it as tit for tat. She has information she is willing to give us, if we can get the charges dropped and stop this IRS audit. It isn't a normal audit," she informed them, glancing among them to see who might be playing both sides of this game. Her people, who she had asked for based on her previous time at the agency, as well as the new ones assigned to her had uncovered some really interesting things, and she could now go in and negotiate with Alice from a position of power. "Whoever is behind this has powerful friends and is out to make Alice Weaver pay."

"Do you know who is behind this?" Director Wolf asked speculatively. He was wondering, not for the first time over the past few days, who the hell Alice Weaver was and why she was so important. It would take weeks, possibly months to get copies of the reports that weren't redacted.

"No, sir. Not yet," she said respectfully, wondering if he knew and wasn't telling her. She trusted Director Wolf. After all, she was working for him. But in this business, it didn't pay to trust anyone completely. It wouldn't be the first time someone in the intelligence community went rogue.

"She'll have to give up her illegally-gotten gains," mentioned one of the agents who had looked at what the IRS had compiled.

"No, that's part of the agreement. She keeps what they are after. They have no proof those gains are illegally gotten, and I think with the alias she used, and they found, she will agree to pay the penalties. That, at least, is something for the IRS to salvage their pride on. This Mr. Smith, who is so gung-ho and has a hard-on for the Weavers, will be losing his job over this snafu he created."

"Why?" several people wanted to know.

Madelyn told of the backhoes and the search that had gone on at the Weaver estate. When Alice found out, she was going to be wild. In the meantime, Kathy Weaver and their teenaged children were probably frightened and upset. Alice Weaver with children...Madelyn had shaken her head over that. She had never thought she'd see that day.

"So, you are just going to give in to all her demands?" someone asked, wondering at this position.

"No, not all. We will negotiate with her, but we want to get that information before the media puts it out there."

"I say lock her up until she gives us all of it," the young agent Alice had verbally torn apart put in, sounding like he was laughing about the situation.

"Do you know what would happen if Alice Weaver was locked up?" Madelyn rounded on the young twit. She waited for him to shake his head. "We would never get one iota of the information we are seeking. The news—TV, paper, and radio—would spread this story far and wide, and the credibility of the United States would be ruined. We don't know what stations have the information or who is waiting for the password, and it might be worldwide for all we know. Based on the names she gave us and what information we now have on them, this could be extremely embarrassing for us."

He looked uncomfortable, but he wasn't down and out. Instead, he foolishly answered with, "There are ways of making people like that talk."

"Get out," Madelyn said, glancing at the man she suspected was the twit's supervisor. "Such talk is foolish! Alice Weaver is a citizen of the United States, and if you read her file," she indicated the thick redacted file they all had copies of, the CliffsNotes version as it were, "you would know she would never give it up. She is bargaining in good faith, and I say we give her what she is asking for. We need this intel to determine how to proceed." She waited as the man left the room, closing the door with a sullen look back at the woman who had embarrassed him.

"You have such faith in her," Director Wolf stated, eyeing Madelyn speculatively and wondering about her relationship with someone he suspected was a criminal. "How do you know that she won't stiff us once we do as she asked? Why can't she give us the information first?"

"This woman was one of the most brilliant minds at Harvard. She didn't even have to go to classes half the time," Madelyn had ascertained

over the years. "She has helped us time and again, and yes, I do have faith in what she says. She's always been honest with us, and she's always cooperated," she indicated the files again. "Would you give up your cards before you got what you wanted? What kind of bargaining chip would she have then?" she asked everyone at the table. She saw several heads nod.

"Then, we arrest her for espionage, conspiracy, and fraud when this is all done?" someone else asked, and Madelyn looked up angrily.

"I don't think you people understand. What she is going to give us won't be all she knows. It's probably the tip of the iceberg, but it will be enough to sink our teeth into and help our investigations. Hell, the names she has already given up have provided you all with plenty to research," she indicated the stacks that were already piling up. "We deal in good faith, and eventually, she might even give us more...*for free.*" A couple of the more senior men and women nodded sagely, hoping that the younger staff would learn from this. You don't go after someone who is providing you with intel you don't have and couldn't have gotten any other way, and you certainly don't go after someone who might have more intel that you desperately need.

"How did she obtain this information?" someone asked, and that led to endless debates about what she might have based only on the names she had given them. Finally, Director Wolf put an end to the speculation, pointing out that they could debate it after they saw what information Alice Weaver had for them. They would decide on a course of action later.

It took many hours, and Alice finally got a good night's sleep. When a disheveled-looking Madelyn knocked and was granted entry into her room, she brought breakfast with her. Over bacon and eggs, she told Alice what she had done.

"Okay, here is a faxed letter of apology from Mr. Smith," she said, holding out the paper for Alice to read. "This is a letter of apology from the IRS, which is forgiving your debt to them, indicating there was a bureaucratic error," she shared a smile with Alice over that wording, "and halting the investigation. There is one penalty," she said apologetically. She showed Alice the one alias that Portia and Andie found that had triggered the red flags with the IRS. "You will have to forfeit that one," she said, sounding sincerely sorry for the blonde. She was uncomfortable immediately as the blonde's eyes glowed yellow. Damn, that again? What was with the lights in this place? She looked up to be sure they were the same fluorescent lights as elsewhere in the building.

"The district attorney in Palos Verdes will be dropping all charges," she said, indicating another fax. "And this gives you immunity from all criminal prosecution, if the data you have for us proves sufficient," she added, knowing her superiors were listening to this conversation and had insisted on that addition.

Alice nodded as she munched on her toast. She waited for Madelyn to finish, swallowed, took a swig of the orange juice, and said, "I want the originals in my hands before I give you what you want."

"Now, wait a minute. These faxes–" Madelyn began.

"Aren't the originals," Alice finished for her, scooping up some eggs with her fork and picking up a piece of bacon.

Sighing, Madelyn knew better than to argue. "How much time do I have left?"

Alice had no idea what date it was as they had kept her isolated, so she asked.

Madelyn was surprised. Alice was usually so on top of such things. Still, it had been a lot of years. She told her the date and the time, and

Alice's usually cat-like eyes opened wide in surprise. She glanced out the window. She had lost a day. "I'd say this evening's news is going to be *very* interesting," she answered blandly, sounding genuinely sad.

"*What?*" Madelyn asked, getting up from her chair in alarm and nearly knocking it over.

Alice shrugged. "I did try to tell your fellow agents that there was a time limit, but they chose to ignore me. By the way, how is my wife?"

Madelyn blinked at the rapid change in conversation. "Your wife is fine. Why?" Did Alice somehow know about the raid on her estate in Palos Verdes?

Alice shrugged again. "I have had a lot of time to think in here," she gestured at the room with its unmade bed.

"It's a lot better than the office they had you in," the CIA operative pointed out.

"It's still not freedom," Alice pointed out in return, and for further emphasis, she pointed to the paperwork. "You also forgot a name."

"A name?"

"Who instigated that?" she indicated the IRS paper.

"Your alias–" she began, but Alice was on to her in an instant.

"Bullshit," she said blandly, and Madelyn smiled, moving in the way of the camera she knew was on them both and putting her back to it, so no one would see her facial expression.

"I'll get back to you," Madelyn promised, giving Alice a look and leaving her own unfinished breakfast to hurry out of the room. Alice's voice stopped her at the door.

"I want you to fax those originals to my lawyers in both New York and Los Angeles, and I want you to show me the printout verifying the faxes," Alice called.

Madelyn nodded to show she had heard. She was surprised Alice hadn't mentioned that tidbit sooner. It made sense. Even if she had the originals in her possession, it wouldn't mean anything if someone else hadn't seen them.

"Cool cucumber, isn't she?" Director Wolf asked from where he had been monitoring the conversation.

"You don't know the half of it," she understated. "We better give her the originals as soon as possible," she suggested, hinting broadly to her superior. She looked pointedly at the clock.

"And if we don't?" he asked, feeling a bit peeved that this Alice, this *nobody,* was basically holding the CIA hostage. He wasn't sure he didn't agree with that young twit about torturing the information out of the woman. There was something here, something *criminal,* and the redacted files alone told him she wasn't someone to be fully trusted. How did she have information on all those Russian criminals?

"Then, sir, you will be responsible for the biggest embarrassment the CIA, and who knows what other government agencies, have suffered in recorded history. This is all going to blow up in your faces."

"You are part of this now," he pointed out angrily.

"Yes, I am *now*, but I have deniability. I haven't been here in years."

"If it tarnishes me and the other agents, it tarnishes you."

Madelyn just smiled, and he wondered what else she was holding back from him, knowing he couldn't ask. He was determined to get Alice Weaver's unaltered file from the archives. "You realize if this gets out there," he gestured beyond the building for emphasis, "she doesn't have a leg to stand on. There will be no deal, and we will hold her until we figure out what she knows on those names."

"Sir, I wouldn't suggest that. You can bet what little she gave us, and you have to admit it is just names at this point, means bupkiss."

"I don't care. She has information we need, and she's blackmailing us to get it."

"You don't know what information she has or doesn't have. She walked in here of her own accord. You can bet someone somewhere knows something about that. She's probably one of the most brilliant women I have ever met."

"I don't care if she's a genius. Something is off with that woman," he responded, feeling uncomfortable for some reason.

"Probably," she agreed, "but she also has information we need and is willing to work out a deal," she wouldn't use the word blackmail as it seemed to feed his fervor in this, "and I say we get the deal brokered for her."

He just smiled slightly, and she knew he wouldn't let this go. "Oh, and by the way, the police asked one more favor. They wonder if somehow, we could stop the virus that is spreading through their computers? Apparently, it's shutting down key systems now, and no one can figure out how to stop it. They can't afford to bring in a whole new system."

"Are you suggesting the CIA step in and stop it?"

"I already have some of our best programmers on it. It's a worm and very sneaky," he answered, sounding annoyed.

Madelyn glanced at the door where Alice Weaver was sitting, and she glanced at the monitor where she saw Alice munching happily on her breakfast...actually, she realized Alice was eating what had been left of her breakfast. Alice's stomach must have returned to normal. That petite woman could *eat*! "Are you suggesting that Ms. Weaver can fix the

worm?" she asked, putting as much incredulity as she could manage into the question.

"Well, did she upload it? Cyber sabotage is a crime too, you know," he reminded her angrily. "If we can prove that...."

"You have supposition, innuendo, and speculation...no hard facts," she pointed out to him, feeling defensive about it. She didn't like being put in the position of having to defend Alice Weaver. They had both read the police file and found nothing to substantiate the officer's outrageous claims. No matter what Alice Weaver had done in the past or in the present, she did have information they needed. Now, they *wanted* the previously unknown information. Those few Russians she had mentioned were powerful men and women, who were now dead, and Madelyn and others wanted to know why and how they died. Accusing Alice without evidence was not something she was prepared to do.

Director Wolf sighed. Getting angry at Madelyn wasn't going to solve the problems and headaches that had arrived with Alice Weaver. There was just too much that wasn't known about the woman. The police chiefs he had spoken with on Madelyn's behalf hadn't been pleased to drop their investigations. One officer had been up in arms about it. Special Agent Linda Miller raved about the things she had heard and transcribed, but all that was moot since there was no proof. Apparently, her evidence had disappeared with the virus. With no tapes, no transcriptions, and only the agent's word, they didn't have anything to arrest Alice Weaver for. Since Agent Miller was just home from the hospital, and it was Alice Weaver that had put the officer in the hospital, it looked like her allegations were simply revenge on the cop's part. "Do you think Alice would help us with the computer worm?" he asked, wondering how much Madelyn really knew about this woman that she wasn't saying.

"Actually, I don't think you want her anywhere near our computers," she put in and then dropped it, not willing to say more.

"Why?"

She shrugged and looked away. Her suspicions, well founded as they were, wouldn't help them anyway. She didn't have the *proof* they required to charge someone like Alice Weaver.

"Madelyn, tell me why?"

"I wouldn't put it past someone to bug our computers. You know the FBI is apparently having problems over on their system, and we share a lot of information with them. We don't want our computers having problems too." The FBI had a *closed system*, which no one on the outside could hack into. The fact that the computers were dealing with something *internal* alarmed many people.

"Are you saying we can't trust Alice Weaver?" he asked, suddenly feeling as though the rug had been pulled out from under his feet after everything they had been going through the past few days.

"I'm saying I wouldn't trust a civilian in our systems," she answered and went silent, waiting for his decisions.

"I have the originals of the faxes in my office," he finally gave in. "Do you think this drive she has will have a bug on it too?"

Madelyn shrugged, but she knew their firewalls and computer people would be watching for it. Just the suggestion of a potential threat would have started alarm bells ringing in their small intelligence community. She went to find the fax numbers for Alice's lawyers, sending the fax copies and all the papers Alice had refused off to New York first, then to Los Angeles. She didn't know that the paperwork sent to New York would have Nia Toyomoto and several senior partners boarding the fastest private jet that could get them to Langley. For Alice's sake, Madelyn also sent the

letters to her office where she now knew Portia Spiros worked, and then, she sent them to Alice's home. She hoped Alice's wife would see everything. She picked up the acknowledgements of the faxes, which would confirm to Alice the receiving fax number, the time, and the number of pages sent.

* * * * *

"Nia Toyomoto to see Alice Weaver," she said as she held up her driver's license to confirm her identity.

"Who?" the security officer asked, taking the license and scanning it into their computer. He was hedging for time by asking her question.

"My client is being held upstairs. Director Wolf and an agent..." she checked one of the faxes to be sure of the name, "Madelyn Korbel...should know what this is about. They will want to see us," she indicated the New York lawyers standing behind her with their identification in their hands. Some didn't have driver's licenses and were using passports.

"And you are?" he asked, reaching for the other IDs to scan them in. At least, they would have a record of who was coming into the building. What security did with the information was beyond his pay grade.

"We're her lawyers," Nia told him quietly, amused at their delay tactics, which seemed so obvious to her.

He glanced at the well-dressed men accompanying their spokeswoman. She was a good-looking woman and was also well-dressed. He would bet their outfits cost more than his monthly salary. "I'll call upstairs and see what I can find out," he promised, reaching for the phone as he continued to scan in the information and hand back the various IDs to the high-

powered attorneys. "Please wait over there," he said, indicating a bank of sofas that looked unused.

"Think they are going to deny she is here?" Stewart Dunham, one of the senior attorneys accompanying her asked. He was due to retire soon but had jumped on this situation once Nia had brought it to the other partners' attention. Alice Weaver was one of their most important clients, and it was imperative that they keep her from being imprisoned for any information the CIA thought she had.

"I don't know. I bet they keep us waiting though," she quipped, wondering how long the wait would be. She had been impressed that the other partners joined her but knew it was mostly because Alice Weaver and the business she had brought their firm through Sasha Brenhov, one of the richest women in the world, was so important to all their well-being. Nia had done most of the legwork in bringing Alice back to life, but that didn't mean the other partners didn't take credit for having her in the firm. Her name, and Sasha Brenhov's name, brought in other business from equally important people. Nia knew one of the only reasons Alice was with their firm was because she had known Alice back in college. She settled down for the wait as the other partners stood or sat, talking quietly as they waited while looking impatiently at their smart phones, which had stopped working properly as they came into this secure building.

"Ms. Toyomoto if you would accompany me?" a lower-level agent finally came to them after a very long while. The lawyers knew their identification had been thoroughly checked to see who they were. They hoped their most impressive credentials would ensure they were treated well, but when the other partners got up to follow, the agent waved them back. "I'm sorry, only Ms. Toyomoto may come up," he told them over their protests and arguments. Security looked up and would have

converged if the agent hadn't waved them back. "Only Ms. Toyomoto," he repeated several times, ignoring the impassioned speeches by the other partners.

"Why only me?" Nia asked curiously as they got on the elevator. She could see her partners, most of them her seniors in the firm, were angry that she was the only one allowed to see their valuable client. They wanted in on this, so they could use their expertise and perhaps earn brownie points for having rushed to Alice's aid. They didn't want Alice Weaver to forget that their firm was there for her onehundred percent. Nia knew that several of these men still thought her much too young and inexperienced to be handling the Weaver and Brenhov files. She shared information and used their expertise when warranted, but Nia was both women's 'go to' lawyer before the cases that came their way, and she earned the firm a lot of money, which was then handed off to the various lawyers and departments within the firm.

"I don't know. I was instructed that you, and *only* you, were to be escorted up," he replied, having no idea why. He followed directions and didn't ask too many questions. It was better that way.

Nia looked about curiously as she was escorted into a private office and introduced to Director Wolf and Madelyn Korbel.

* * * * *

When Director Wolf went with Madelyn to hand Alice the original, signed paperwork, Alice was surprised and pleased to see Nia Toyomoto accompanying them.

"Hello, Nia," she said with a smile.

"Well, Alice, as I live and breathe. Nice to know you are really alive and not just on the paperwork I filed," Nia said with a smile, having handled the intricate and delicate wording of bringing Alice back to life in previous months. "What have you gotten yourself into that requires you to have immunity?" she asked, sitting down and indicating the papers.

"Is it all in order?" Alice asked blandly, amused with her lawyer. She knew Nia was now an important partner of the law firm in New York. At Nia's nod, she looked them over, folded them neatly, and sat back, her arms crossed. She glanced at the fax acknowledgements and the various numbers they had been sent to, nodding coldly to Madelyn and waiting.

"Is there no way you would have done this simply as a citizen and out of the goodness of your heart?" the director asked as he looked at Alice Weaver. He detested her hair, which was sticking up all over, messed up further by her fingers running through it as it dried after her shower. He could mentally see her in grunge clothing, something he abhorred. His own impeccable suit was like a uniform, and he was judging her on her appearance. Nia and Madelyn both knew that was a mistake.

"Oh, but I assure you, Director, I am a good citizen," Alice informed him, glancing at Nia, who had stiffened at the tone he used on her client. She hadn't liked the short meeting in his office. He was an arrogant ass, and she knew Alice enjoyed deflating such people. This didn't bode well, and she only hoped her firm's expertise would get her client out of this mess.

"Well, then where is the information you promised me?"

"You? It's for the American people," she corrected, antagonizing him and seeing Madelyn turning aside slightly, almost as though to hide her laughter. Nia grinned, not caring if the man saw it. She too could appreciate the hairs Alice was splitting. Whatever Alice had done, Nia

would defend her with her dying breath. "And when I get everything I asked–" she began, but he interrupted.

"We gave you everything you asked for!" he thundered. "Where the hell is our information? We gave you that," he slapped at the paperwork, "in good faith. Where is your good faith?"

Alice deliberately looked at his watch, surprised that anyone wore a watch anymore with the proliferation of cell phones. "Tick tock, Director. The evening news will need some time to process it, but I wonder how many of the stations will really vet that information before broadcasting it?"

He leaned over the table in front of her, trying to intimidate her. "If one word of that information gets out, I'll throw you in prison and throw away the key."

"You aren't trying to intimidate my client, are you?" Nia put in, but it was too late.

Alice rose abruptly, the top of her head hitting his jutting jaw and closing it painfully as they collided. "If you knew where I'd been the past few years, you would know nothing you can do to me could be worse than that," she spat defiantly in his face where he was already nursing a painful jaw.

"Then we will go after your–"

"Don't finish that sentence, Director. Trust me, you don't want to finish it," Madelyn interrupted loudly enough to drown out what he had been about to say. She could see the lawyer was ready to do battle. "Ms. Weaver has complied, and we have complied," she indicated the paperwork. "I promise to get you that name," she looked earnestly in Alice's glowing, orange eyes. She realized the color wasn't a trick of the light, and Alice's eyes were orange. This woman was very dangerous.

She had had her suspicions about this woman before based on some of the reports she had read over the years, but she felt the current information and accusations of Special Agent Linda Miller plus other suspicions confirmed it. Madelyn's training instinctively told her the look in this woman's eye meant Alice Weaver was a killer. She would have taken a step back if she wasn't preparing to defend her superior. He had no idea the mine field he had been about to step into.

Alice looked at Madelyn, glanced at Nia, and calmed down. She was very, very angry, and she was tired of being held here. She nodded slightly, agreeing to Madelyn's terms. She trusted that the agent's word was her bond, and Madelyn would get the information or pay Alice's price. She rubbed the top of her head where it had collided with the director's jaw, then she used her fingernail to slit the skin on the webbing between her thumb and forefinger, peeling it back.

Madelyn, Nia, and the director stared in fascinated horror as she removed a bloody microchip that looked amazingly like a slimmed down, smaller SIM card that could be found in any cell phone. She held it up between her nails. As the director went to take it from her, she pulled her hand back, looked at him angrily, and handed the microchip deliberately to Madelyn.

"I'll expect that information from you shortly," Alice told her as she watched the agent close her fingers on the chip. She appreciated the tissue the agent handed her to staunch the flow of blood from her hand and used it to clean her fingernail as well.

"You understand, I have to review this?" she said, indicating the chip in her fist.

"Of course. You have…" she looked again at the director's watch, "two hours."

"Can't you stop it?" she asked, worried that they wouldn't have enough time.

Alice smiled, and it looked rather sinister. "Not unless I'm released from here. I must have time to get back to my hotel."

"We've already–" began the director before he caught himself.

Alice turned her smile on the man, her orange eyes glowing. She didn't say a word as Madelyn hurried out.

Hearing her leave, the director turned and left the room. "Watch her," he said unnecessarily in a low aside to the pair of armed guards outside the door. He looked back at Alice, who was still smiling, before he hurried away, and the door shut.

"Care to explain what is going on?" Nia asked, watching as Alice sat back and refused to answer her. She sighed. Apparently, Alice didn't *need* her. She knew the other partners would begrudge her the time alone with this woman. Alice Weaver was a significant and profitable client and had brought them Sasha Brenhov, one of the richest women, if not the richest women, in the world. Their business had increased exponentially since these two women had used the services of their firm. Would the partners mind that they had come here to Virginia for nothing? Probably not.

* * * * *

"We should arrest her now," he mumbled as he hurried to the tech room where Madelyn had run off to. And she had run, despite her high heels.

"You'll have a hard time arresting her with that letter she has in her hands," Madelyn mumbled as she heard him enter the room. She knew the

reputation of the firm Nia Toyomoto worked for and knew she could make real trouble for the authorities if her client wasn't released. The various partners that had accompanied the woman had ties to some very powerful people worldwide. The politicians alone that these men and women knew could and would create headaches that reminded her of her own political ousting years ago.

"I have a chip, and I need the information off it immediately," she called out, watching as the nerds and geeks, who loved this part of their job, clamored for the odd little chip.

"We're going to need a password," one of the techs announced.

"Shit!" Director Wolf ejaculated under his breath.

"I'll be right back," Madelyn said as she quickly left the room and ran up the stairs that separated it from an observation platform that ran around the entire room. She could see the director was angry with Alice's behavior, but she really didn't blame the woman. The CIA wasn't known to be trustworthy, and he would have double-crossed Alice if he could...he still would.

"Get a tap on the hotel room where Alice Weaver is staying," he ordered once Madelyn was out of the room.

"Won't we need–" began one of the newer techs, but he was shushed by a look from another tech, who immediately got on the order, reaching for his computer. If the director ordered it, they wouldn't need any other authorization.

Of course, Alice's room had already been tossed for information that could be used against her. She had planned for that. She was just lying in the room they had provided her, waiting for someone to come for the password. They hadn't asked for the password, and she hadn't volunteered that information. She didn't care. She had her get out of jail

free cards in the forms they had given her. She looked at the fax acknowledgements and recognized her home number and her office numbers. She could only speculate that the numbers following the Los Angeles and New York area codes belonged to her lawyers' offices. If they really had copies of the forms that were now in her possession, she had corroborating evidence. She knew Nia must have gotten her copy, or she wouldn't have been here. Still, she didn't say a word to the Eurasian woman who stood patiently looking out the window from the very same spot Alice had stood in not so long ago. Nia was enjoying the view of the beautiful Virginia countryside outside the window.

A knock on the door had her looking up and over as it opened. Madelyn stuck her head in. "Password?" she asked without preamble, giving Alice a look that had them both trying to keep from laughing.

"Kazakhstan," she answered. "Good luck spelling it; it's a bugger." Alice laughed, knowing they had already gotten the chip inserted into their computers. She wondered when the worm that was in it would make itself known. *Worms*, she corrected herself.

Madelyn hurried back to the tech room and announced, "Kazakhstan," as she entered and saw the techs working on the card. The amount of information this tiny card could hold amazed and alarmed them as they began to print it out and analyze it. Madelyn called her team in to help, separating out various documents as they came up.

"We've got a bug," someone called. They had been expecting it as per the director's orders.

"See? We can't *trust* her," Director Wolf angrily aimed that one at Madelyn.

"Of course, we can. She gave us all this. You couldn't expect her not to try the bug," she reasoned as she looked at some particularly interesting

pictures of the military equipment that had to be in Kazakhstan. What did this equipment have to do with the dead men and women who had been part of the Russian mafia?

"Another password," the tech announced as they started trying variations of the original password, deliberate misspellings, and even Alice's name.

"Try Russia," Madelyn suggested as she looked at the stack of intel they already had before them. This information more than paid for Alice's freedom. She moved to go and tell her, and Director Wolf stopped her.

"Where are you going?" he asked, looking up from some of the bloody pictures he now had in his possession, along with Russian newspaper articles that told of these people's deaths. They would have to bring in some of their bilingual people to interpret the Russian script.

"I'm going to release Alice Weaver, so she can call off the press before *this*," she gestured at the mound of paperwork stacking up, some of it very sensitive information, "gets out there."

He really badly wanted to stop her, but he felt his hands were tied. Alice Weaver had delivered. How she had obtained all this information, including financial information, he did not know. He learned from her file that she claimed to have been kidnapped last year with Sasha Brenhov, and he assumed it had to do with her. They would need to have more conversations. He needed to know more, despite their agreement. Private citizen or no, he must see her redacted file. He felt it was bullshit how she had been accorded special privileges! It was obvious she knew a lot more than she was telling.

* * * * *

"Ms. Weaver can go," Madelyn told the guards, who nodded. She opened the door and saw Alice gazing out the window with Nia. The two of them were laughing together as they chatted. "I have your clothes here," she said, looking down at the small pile of Alice's laundered clothes in her hands. "Shall I arrange to have a car out front to take you to your hotel?"

"Thank you," Alice said, glancing around and wondering what time it was. She glanced at Nia, who had been reminiscing with her.

"You still have half an hour," Madelyn told her as she put the clothes down and started to leave.

"Madelyn," Alice stopped her. When the older woman turned to look at the blonde, she said, "We both know this won't be the end of it. He will want more."

Madelyn nodded. "All I can do is try to rein him in. I hope he will be satisfied with what you gave us."

"He won't be," Alice said as she began to pull off her shoes and socks, stepping down on the heels of both to pull them off.

Madelyn nodded again, turned, and left the room. She knew Alice was right, and Director Wolf would want more. He would want to drain all knowledge from Alice until she was dry, and even then, he wouldn't believe that she had given him everything.

"Will you give them more?" Nia asked, turning to give Alice her back and some privacy.

"I have no idea," Alice admitted.

* * * *

The decoy worm was easily killed in the system, but the other worm, rather *worms* that lay dormant within the layers of data they were going through were eager to work their way through the system in a less obvious fashion. They would pass the most comprehensive scans the super tech computers could throw at them. Even the most in-depth and destructive scans designed specifically to search for worms such as this would miss many of them because they weren't active. They would be activated…in time. They would be triggered by the actual scans searching for them, some in months and others perhaps not for years.

"Holy shit!" the analysts said time and again as they looked over the information Alice Weaver had provided the CIA.

"Do you have someone tailing her?" Director Wolf asked one of his men when he saw that Agent Korbel was perusing the stack of intel they had gotten off the disk.

"No need. Madelyn had a car take her back to the hotel."

"On that tap?" he asked another agent, who assured him it was in place.

* * * * *

Alice didn't *go* to her room. Her hotel had a payphone in the lobby, something that wasn't seen too often these days. She went to the payphone instead, and using a credit card she had memorized, she punched in a phone number, waited for an answer, and began typing in numbers, deliberately typing too fast for the men watching her as she also shifted from side to side to block her hand from their view. She paused, listened, then hung up the phone and went to her room where she began to pick up the mess the agents had left in the room. Nia followed her. Having given her the privacy she needed for her phone call she didn't ask any questions.

The other partners had wanted to question Alice and let her know they were there for her, but she had gotten in Madelyn's car with Nia *only* and had left the rest of them to their own devices. Nia had waved her cell phone, a silent promise that she would be in contact. Taking a cab to the airport, Alice was able to get a ride on a private jet service back to Los Angeles, and Nia met up with the partners and headed back to New York. The lawyer was feeling particularly useless but had been pleased to see her old friend alive and well, even if she was up to something that Nia might have difficulty extracting her from. The other partners were particularly miffed that they hadn't been allowed to question their client. The flight back to New York was quite uncomfortable for Nia.

Alice's junker was parked in the carpark she and Kathy had been using to throw off would-be followers, so she headed directly there. She was shocked when she recognized Kathy's Lexus exactly where she had left it. She searched to find where she had hidden the key, found it, and got in to head for Palos Verdes, all the while wondering at her reception.

* * * * *

"I want you out! This is *it*, Alice; *this* is my limit. I want a divorce, and this time I'm not screwing around. I told Portia just today that I was done."

Alice was shocked when Kathy met her in the garage with this edict. "Didn't Portia get the fax? Didn't you?"

"Yes, I saw that you stopped the investigations. I even saw the apologies. I checked and confirmed all the accounts are unfrozen, but that doesn't mean anything to me. I want you out and gone. I can't deal with this shit anymore…it's never-ending. No matter what we have done or

what you have said, it just keeps coming at us. I want the divorce, and I want out of this." Kathy was waving her arms passionately.

Alice looked at her sadly for a moment, contemplating, and then she nodded. The hair sticking up on the top of her hair made her look even more intense. "All right, Kathy, whatever you want," she told her wearily. "I still love you, you know?"

"I know, Alice," Kathy told her sadly, surprised at her easy acquiescence. "I love you too, but it's not enough. I can't keep going through these dramas forever."

Alice already knew that the house was probably in sad shape because she'd seen the state of the yard. She was furious and would lodge a complaint demanding that whoever was responsible should pay for the damage. In the meantime, she would pay to have her home and yard restored, at least for the children's sake. "May I get my clothes?"

"I've already packed for you. Do you want me to call a cab or an uber?"

"Call a cab. May I see the kids?"

"I won't ever keep you from our children," Kathy vowed in a small, sad voice, feeling her heart breaking. It wasn't the first time. This woman had broken her heart many times, and there wasn't much left unbroken.

"Mom!" Emily greeted her enthusiastically. "I thought you had gone forever," she said dramatically, throwing herself into Alice's arms.

"Naw, I had to go get this crap with the IRS straightened out," she told her, giving her as enthusiastic a hug as the teen gave her. She was pleased that her little girl was filling out after her long illness. It was even possible the teen was growing taller.

"It really sucked; those cops were really mean," Sean told her, following her into the master bedroom that Kathy had cleaned up in the days since the raid.

"Some are like that but not all of them," Alice told him, unable to be a cop hater despite what they had done. She picked up the cases Kathy had packed for her.

"Are you going somewhere?" Emily asked.

"Mom has asked me for a divorce, so I'm going to have to find a place to live. Now, not like that," she said, silencing the teen's argument. "I've put your mom through a lot, and it's not fair to any of us. I just want to know you guys are safe and happy. You can come visit me when I find a place," she promised. "At least we all know I'm alive," she joked, holding up the cell phone she had turned back on, only to find dozens of texts from her family. Some of the message had become increasingly hostile as Kathy got angrier.

"She shouldn't treat you like that," Emily said, defending Alice.

"Em, your mother and I love each other," Alice started, seeing beyond the two teens to where Kathy was unashamedly listening in the hallway outside the room.

"Then you'll get back together?" she asked hopefully.

Alice shrugged and shook her head regretfully. "I don't think so, baby. I think this time she's had enough. We both love you guys." She glanced up at their much taller son and smiled to include him. "You have to understand that sometimes relationships simply do not work out, and it's no one's fault. I will always love your mom. I'm certain she loves me too. I love you guys, and that will never change."

"I don't want you to leave," Em insisted. She was too old to stamp her foot, but she felt like doing it.

"And I don't want to leave you, baby but think how much fun it will be to shop for another place," she said, her words sounding weak to both their ears. Sean grinned but it was half-hearted at best. "You'll visit?" Alice asked the growing teen.

Sean nodded, sniffing suspiciously.

Alice picked up her bags, slinging one around her neck. Sean leaned over and carried several out for her, and Em grabbed a couple too. Kathy quickly ducked down the stairs, so the teens wouldn't see her. She'd already ordered a taxi for Alice. She wanted her gone. She and Mrs. Fernandez, along with Portia and Andie, had spent days getting the house in livable order. There were things that needed repair, and Portia had told her to keep the receipts. Already, they were closing the office. They no longer needed it since Alice had stopped the investigations and was here to take the reins of her business. Portia was sending out inquiries to law firms in Los Angeles, and Andie was thinking of moving out of state and looking for a position elsewhere.

The kids helped tuck Alice into her cab, and she ordered the driver to take her to the Ritz-Carlton where she was able to get a room. She looked sadly about the luxurious room, her luggage piled forlornly in the closet, waiting to be unpacked. She wasn't happy to be separated from Kathy and her children again. She sighed. Kathy was right; they had been through a lot. She was tired too. She wondered why Sebastian's men hadn't gotten her family out as planned?

The next day, Alice shopped for and bought herself a car but not the Porsche she had always favored. She decided to splurge a bit. After all, it was time to get a decent car, and the old junker certainly wouldn't do. She donated the junker to a charity, and they picked it up, not even realizing the name on the title was someone else's as they took it away. She was

thrilled as she test-drove and enjoyed the feel of the Ferrari 488 that she eventually purchased. She knew her children would be thrilled, especially Sean, who was always looking at expensive sports cars. She had known she could remain unobtrusive with her Porsche. After all, they were much more common in Los Angeles than the Ferrari, but she felt justified. It was a similar blue to Kathy's own Lexus. She loved the convertible and eagerly drove it, making sure to stay within the speed limit despite the temptation to push it.

"Mrs. Weaver I'm so glad you called!" Charlotte, the realtor, told her when she arrived at her office a few days later. It was the same realtor who had sold them the property in Palos Verdes, and she was anxious to accommodate this client again. Alice had told her she was about to become single and needed a place of her own. She didn't want one by the marina as she had been there when she and Kathy first married, and no, she wouldn't be selling the house in Palos Verdes. That house would go to Kathy for the children. Alice didn't need the money.

With all the listings Charlotte showed her, Alice was quickly on the way to owning a nice, small house on the beach in Malibu. It was a little ways from Palos Verdes—they had to cross Manhattan Beach and Santa Monica—but Alice loved the feel of the place. When she eventually showed her new house and car to her children, they were ecstatic. There had been a beach where they could walk down from the bluffs around the house in Palos Verdes, but it wasn't really a user-friendly beach, and this one was fantastic. When they found out which stars lived along this stretch of Alice's beach, they were thrilled.

"Spending a lot of money these days, aren't you?" Kathy asked when Alice came to retrieve the computers the police had returned. Sean was happy to get the gaming computer back, but Alice told him it should go to

Malibu, so he had something to play there too. He was reluctant to let it go until she promised she would get another computer for him to set up at the Palos Verdes house, and she promised he could go with her to pick it out. She didn't tell him why she wanted his gaming computer for now.

"You know, for once in my life, I'm going to indulge," Alice told her. "There's plenty for you. I've already told my lawyers to give you the house and all the money in the bank accounts."

"You know I don't want your money," Kathy said, hurt as she watched Sean carefully pack the computer into the Ferrari. There wasn't a lot of cargo space in the low-slung vehicle.

"Yes, Kathy, I know that," Alice said sadly. She wanted to caution Kathy about saying anything but knew that would only piss her off. She could trust Kathy not to say anything.

"Linda contacted me," Kathy told her, looking at Alice. She was feeling bad about instigating the divorce Portia had already filed on her behalf. Alice was being beyond generous and beyond reasonable, giving her more than the fifty percent of the assets she was due, and that annoyed her more than if Alice had fought the divorce.

"Yeah? What'd she want?"

"She was going to sue, but Portia sent a copy of the video over to her lawyers and threatened something about illegal prosecution...those papers you faxed us?"

Alice nodded but didn't say a word. It was better to let the past remain there. She was done. Her marriage to this woman was over. "Well, I've got to go. You should come and see the house sometime."

"I'll let Sean drive the car, and he can bring Emily," Kathy compromised. She didn't want to see Alice's new house. The children raving about the new house hurt her for some reason. She did appreciate

that Alice had sent landscapers over to restore their yard. It had taken weeks, but already, the new sod was taking root. Some of the flowers would take years to recover.

Alice understood. Making a break like this was hard, but it was necessary. She waved as she went down the stairs, the older computers in her car would have to go to someone who could recycle the parts. The gaming computer would go in her new den. She had some messages she had waited weeks to send, and she could only send them through that computer. She knew the police hadn't been able to find anything, but that was only because they hadn't thought about the fact that people could send messages through the games. They hadn't thought that someone like Alice would even *play* such games. Alice played games alright…just not the kind that were contained on a mere computer.

* * * * *

Alice was surprised to find Kathy on her doorstep a week later. "Someone killed Linda Miller!" she accused, looking at Alice with hard eyes.

~The End~   K'Anne ;-P

If you have enjoyed **MANDATING MALICE**, I hope you will enjoy this excerpt from

INN THE DOG HOUSE

Life has gone to the dogs for Charlie Abella. Years of showing champion Border Collies has left her feeling burned out. Moving on with her life, she heads to college and then takes on the world of business. She is blessed to find a job working in sales for the pet industry where her knowledge and skills will help her move quickly up the corporate ladder and away from the small town of Searsport, Maine where she grew up. When she loses a beloved relative, Charlie returns to Searsport for the funeral, believing now, she can finally cut all ties to her hometown.

Charlie's only regret about moving away was leaving behind her favorite aunt. Aunt Kitty had been her champion and her anchor when she felt her own family didn't understand her. Kitty saw herself in her young niece and understood Charlie as no one else could, so it was only natural she would choose to make her favorite niece her heir. Sadly, she knows only too well that Charlie's family will disapprove no matter how Charlie decides to use the money she inherits.

Reagan has been left on her own to raise two children. Possessing few business skills, she is forced to take on a series of dead-end jobs that barely allow her to make ends meet. Reagan has only her faith and her children to provide solace and support. When Reagan encounters a woman dog walker on the street, she takes some comfort in feeling 'at least she is better off than a woman with too many dogs to handle.'

Inexplicably, fate constantly causes the two women to bump into each other, and when Reagan feels herself becoming attracted to the woman, she is confused. Unlike Charlie, Reagan is not a lesbian, and she is frightened by her feelings for this woman. Will Reagan eventually act on her attraction, or will she continue to resist it?

The dogs know what is right for this couple. Now, if only the humans would listen!

CHAPTER ONE

The judge's voice rang out, "One…two…three…four," as the judge pointed to each dog and handler, and the audience began to applaud her choices.

Charlie was thrilled, and she and Royal Rufus Von Brookstone, Roy-Boy for short, began to dance. He knew he had won when he heard, "Good boy," directed at him. He jumped up into Charlie's arms, and she laughed merrily as he wiggled his little body joyfully, panting happily as he shared in her pleasure. With that win, he had become grand champion for the third time and would retire shortly. Aunt Kitty would be pleased. Charlie put Roy-Boy down, and he wagged his entire body happily as she went to shake the judge's hand politely after the others had received their ribbons. Afterward, they had their pictures taken with the judge. Charlie brushed the shavings from her dress and put Roy-Boy into a classic showman's pose. His legs were back and his body leaning forward…Hell, he was so smart he could do this by himself. Charlie whipped out a comb to fuss at his hair, the feathers on his legs puffing out beautifully. He smiled prettily for the camera when the poses relaxed; he knew how to ham it up. Taking her trophy and purple ribbon, Charlie headed out of the ring and straight towards where their grooming table was set up.

"Another win, Charlotte?" someone said cattily; they were obviously jealous. Charlie ignored the woman, not liking her or the dogs she bred and showed. The dogs, like their owner, always ended up being nasty.

"Good for you, Charlie, and you too, Roy-Boy!" others said, complimenting them on all their hard work. Charlie accepted their words as her due and thanked her admirers. Roy-Boy knew he was being complimented too. His tail was up, and his hips were swaying from side to side as he trotted along at her side, showing off.

"Up," she ordered him, and with very little effort he jumped to the platform of the grooming table and tried to give her a kiss. "No kisses," she laughingly commanded while dodging his agile tongue as he got in one celebratory lick. He knew he'd done good. Charlie began to pack up the few supplies she had left out, replacing the comb she'd carried in her pocket to touch him up in the ring. She gave him a treat, which he gratefully took and immediately ate, chomping loudly.

"Well, when are the rest of us going to have a chance?" a voice asked as she started stacking her boxes.

Charlie looked up at Trina and smiled. "Now. This was Roy-Boy's last show," she told her.

"No!" she gasped. "Really?"

At Charlie's nod, she asked, "What about you? Are you going to show any more of your aunt's dogs or are you branching out?"

"Nope, this was my last show too. I'm done with this," she gestured towards the large Cumberland County Civic Center where the Portland Dog Club had held its show.

"But why? You're so good at this!"

"I'm kinda sick of it. I've been doing it since I was nine, and Aunt Kitty promised if I got Roy-Boy his championship, then we could retire together. I don't need the stress, and..." she lowered her voice, so no one would overhear, "I'm sick of these bitches," she indicated the women whose catty remarks always seemed to arise from their bitterness over their own failures.

Trina laughed at the pun as was expected. She understood though. Starting in 4-H, Charlie had been showing her own dogs and then, her aunt's dogs for the last decade. She had learned from some of the best trainers available, and now, she was a great trainer herself. She deserved to retire while she was on top.

"You've earned it too, haven't you Roy-Boy?" she crooned, dodging his nose and more kisses as he responded to her voice. His tail was flying high as he acknowledged her question. She was certain he understood what she was saying.

"Is your aunt going to breed him?" Trina asked, knowing the gossips would want to know, and she already knew a couple people who would jump at the chance to breed their own bitches to the triple champion.

"Yes. She's already bred him to her own bitches, but I'm sure she'd consider other offers," Charlie answered. "Down, Roy," she told him, and he hopped adroitly off the grooming table. Although she knew she didn't have to worry about him running away, she stepped on his leash as she collapsed the grooming table on casters. She quickly stacked the boxes of grooming supplies on the table.

"I'll miss seeing you around. What are you going to do?"

"I'm going to college next semester, and I'll be around," Charlie answered, feeling confident. She was looking forward to getting out of

Maine and going to school in Massachusetts. She was tired of small towns where everyone knew everyone else's business. At nineteen, she thought herself very worldly. She packed up the family station wagon and let Roy into the front seat, cranking the window halfway down, so he could poke his nose out in the fresh air. It took no time at all to lift the grooming boxes into the back and then put the table upside down on top of them, so it wouldn't roll while she drove. Shutting the tailgate, she got behind the wheel. Roy leaned over to snuffle her, trying to get in one last kiss as she pushed him back to his side of the car. She placed the trophy on the floor in front of him, wrapped the ribbon around it, and smiled.

"Grand champion, old boy, and you deserve it too!" she said to the dog, cupping his muzzle fondly, giving him a quick kiss, and releasing him as she started up the station wagon. While letting the car warm up for a few moments, she pushed a button to roll up the back window, already smelling the carbon monoxide from the tail pipe seeping into the car. She cranked her own window down to get a cross breeze and carefully drove off the grass of the parking lot, bouncing her way along as she avoided other participants, vendors, and the many spectators. Reaching over with her free hand, she yanked on the rubber band holding her arm band and number until it gave way. She threw that on the floor in front of the trophy, chuckling silently—the number sixty-nine appealed to her macabre sense of humor.

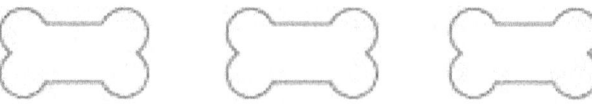

"Well, Aunt Kitty, you got what you wanted. Roy-Boy here is a three-time grand champion," Charlie announced, letting the champion precede her into the old, Victorian house. She smiled at her aunt, who greeted the dog, allowing him to kiss all over her face as she praised him for all *his* hard work. Charlie placed the large trophy on the TV, so her aunt could admire it. The ribbon looked bright and cheerful against its rich gold cup.

"That's Royal Rufus Von Brookstone," she corrected and then smiled at her niece, pleased that she had won this final championship for her. She painfully rose from where she had been sitting, using her cane as she dodged the three other dogs who had come to greet Roy. "Thank you, Charlotte. I really do appreciate everything you have done with the dogs. I guess you'll be packing up now and heading to Boston?"

Charlie nodded. "I have another week before school starts, but I'll be back for Thanksgiving, maybe even Halloween," she promised her aunt, leaning in to give her a hug.

"I don't know why you have to go so far away," she complained. "We have perfectly good schools here in Maine," she pointed out prissily.

Charlie pulled back to look at her aunt to see if she was serious. Seeing the twinkle in her aunt's eyes, she laughed. She was parroting her stodgy sister, Charlie's mother, when she said such things. "Tsk, tsk," Charlie admonished the older woman she adored so. Of all the things she would miss when she got out of Searsport, she would miss her Aunt Kitty the most. Her whole life, she'd only ever heard her mother refer to her sister by her formal first name, Catherine. Everyone else referred to her aunt as Kitty, which was kind of ironic since she had bred and shown champion Border Collies for as long as Charlie could remember. Out of the corner of her eye, she spotted a cat eyeing her from the steps. She smiled at the large feline, pleased to see it make an appearance. The dogs eyed it too, hoping for a chase, but they wouldn't be satisfied by this particular cat. She'd often made it known they weren't to bother her with such undignified things, backing them up with well-aimed smacks of her paws against tender dog noses and using her claws as a last resort.

"I'm gonna miss you around here, Puddin," Kitty told the young woman. She meant it too. Of all her many nieces and nephews, Charlotte was certainly her favorite. They shared a love of animals, more specifically, a love of training and showing dogs. She understood the girl more than she realized. She especially understood the pull of the big city, but she also knew that someday, the pull of home would bring her back to this section of Maine and her family. It had happened to her too. She'd married a good man and been widowed far too young. Life had thrown many challenges at her, and she still wasn't satisfied with what it had given her.

Charlie quickly unpacked her gear from her parents' station wagon, the same one she would use to head for Boston and her dorm the following week. She neatly stacked the boxes in her aunt's familiar garage, setting the portable grooming table on its side against a wall. She admired the full grooming area of the two-car garage for a moment. The set-up reminded her a lot of her aunt: neat and modern. Then, she looked up at the Queen Anne Victorian house her aunt owned and shook her head at the contradictions. Her aunt was a rebel in a family that didn't appreciate rebels. She was the odd one out. Maybe that was why Charlie loved her so, even more than her own parents. No one knew that, but she hoped Aunt Kitty at least suspected. Kitty had never had children of her own, but with the five children

Charlie's parents had borne and her brother Peter's family, she was well-supplied with snow shovelers and grass cutters that could take care of their now elderly aunt.

Charlie waved as she pulled out of her aunt's drive. She saw Aunt Kitty looking out the window, but she was too far away to see the sad look in the woman's eyes. Charlie headed for her own home in Searsport, the next town out of Belfast.

CHAPTER TWO

Charlie got out of her brand-new Mazda Miata. She smiled at the convertible, giving it an imaginary polish with the side of her hand as she admired the gleaming, red paintwork. She looked up at the porch of Aunt Kitty's Victorian, pleased to see the elderly woman waiting there for her, three dogs at heel on her left and one on the right. The dog on her right had earned his special space; he was now fifteen. She glanced at the round cupola on the corner of the house and spotted a cat looking out the window at her suspiciously.

"That's a pretty spiffy car you got there, Puddin," her aunt commented, amused by the sports car her niece was driving. She already knew her sister, Margaret didn't approve. She'd heard her worrying about the fast people that her daughter associated with through her work. She worried that at twenty-nine years of age, the young woman wasn't married and hadn't made her a grandmother, unlike all her siblings. Kitty had tried to tell her to let the child be, to let her have her family in her own time, but Margaret wouldn't listen to her. Kitty was so different from Margaret and their brother, Peter. The differences were like night and day, but then, she'd always been the rebel, despite growing up in the same time and era as them.

"Yep, just bought it last month," Charlie bragged, pleased with herself as she walked up the steps to the house. Leaning down, she gave her aunt a kiss on the cheek and a firm hug at the same time. She released her with a smile, making sure she was secure with her cane, then leaned down and greeted each of the four dogs individually. For as long as she had known her aunt, she had kept at least four dogs in her house. The village had tried to limit her to only three, but because she was a registered breeder of champion Border Collies, she had often kept more, many more than they normally allowed. The village couldn't seem to do anything about the eccentric, old woman because she'd been grandfathered in when they passed the ordinance about how many dogs you could keep within the city limits.

"Hey, there, old man. How are you doing, Roy-Boy?" she asked the old dog, remembering their adventures together over the years. He was still a viable dog, but now, he had white whiskers. He still tried to give her a kiss. "No kisses," she protested automatically, pushing away the persistent tongue and snout of the dog.

"And who is that?" Aunt Kitty asked, seeing a posh-looking dog sitting in the passenger seat.

Charlie looked back over her shoulder, although she knew who it was. She smiled at the vision of the black and white Poodle sitting in the front seat, wearing Doggles brand dog sunglasses and laughing as she panted towards them. She looked interested in the four dogs Charlie had greeted, and Charlie got the impression if she were able, she would have lowered her Doggles and looked them over like any snooty girl. "*That*, Aunt Kitty, is one of the models from our shoot.

Her owner died, and rather than let her go to the pound, I asked if I could have her. Careful. She's sensitive," she warned with a laugh. Cara wasn't sensitive in the least. She barely missed her former owner as she was paraded from photo shoot to photo shoot, making money for her owner with her good looks. She was trimmed within an inch of her French cut. Charlie planned to let it all grow out and then shape it into a sporty cut. She signaled the dog, who hesitated only a second before jumping out of the car, her paws never touching the red paint job as she landed easily on the sidewalk and made her way up the walk, prancing. Her French cut, with the balls around her ankles and above bare toes and painted nails, made her look very posh.

"Oh, my. She does have style, doesn't she?" Aunt Kitty asked, smiling at the dog that was clearly showing off for the other dogs.

"Aunt Kitty, Roy-Boy, Bonner, Bandit, and Leon, this is Cara," she said by way of introductions.

"That isn't Leon. Leon passed. That's Two-Tone," her aunt hissed, almost as though Charlie had personally insulted the brown and white dog.

"Oh, I'm terribly sorry, Two-Tone," she said formally to the Border Collie. He eyed her before looking back at the dog wearing goggles. It was clear where his interest lay, and he hadn't cared in the least that she got his name wrong. "Let's get these off, so you can see her pretty eyes," Charlie said as she whipped the Doggles off, careful not to catch the curly hair of the Poodle's topknot in the sunglasses' rubber band at the back.

The dogs reached out as far as they dared without leaving the porch without permission, trying to scent the new dog. They glanced meaningfully at Aunt Kitty, but she ignored the dogs and took a step down to greet the fancy Poodle. "My, aren't you a beauty," she murmured, sitting down painfully with her cane between her legs, so she'd be on the same level when the dog approached.

Cara sniffed the new woman, sensing something about her that she immediately accepted. It was a hint of something only a dog brain could detect. She not only sensed that this dog lady was acceptable, but that there was a part of her that was part of Charlie, who Cara had given her whole heart to. Charlie gave her more attention and steady, no-nonsense direction than her last owner, who had only yelled at her to go here and go there and gave her treats only when she performed. Charlie was fair but firm and repeatedly played with her. Cara adored Charlie's giddy sense of humor.

After a good petting, Aunt Kitty let Cara pass her to greet the other dogs. She didn't want any nonsense with posturing and territorial squabbles. Her gang knew better. Kitty had had many dogs in and out of the house over the years—some that stayed while she trained them and others who came only to be bred. She'd retired Roy-Boy from breeding three years ago. He'd had a good go, and his pups were worth a fortune. Bonner was one of his sons and worth almost as much as Roy-Boy. Bonner had already won his second championship with a different trainer since Charlotte had refused to train or show again.

"How's the job?" Kitty asked her favorite niece knowingly as they watched the dogs poke and prod each other, tails wagging like crazy as they became acquainted. She was pleased to see this Poodle's tail wasn't docked. Its long hair made the tail appear like a flag, much like her Border Collies' tails.

"You were right," she conceded with a smile. "I'm having a ball." They both grinned at the double entendre.

"I'm so pleased," Kitty smiled in return, extending her hand to the tall brunette as she rose painfully from the steps.

Charlie held firm to her aunt's hand, letting her do most of the pulling as she got up. Once she was steady on her feet with her cane propping her up, Charlie let go but was prepared to catch her if she lost her balance. After a second, she climbed onto the porch and gestured for Charlie to join her as she made her way to one of the swings on the wide porch.

"How long have you been there now?"

"Three years. I'm maxing out what I can do with them unless they expand. I don't think they'll expand, but I learned a lot."

"How'd you like that trade show in Las Vegas?" her aunt asked, knowingly.

"Oh, that was awesome! I saw the coolest things," she enthused, remembering the massive aisles of products and services related to the pet industry.

"Maybe, when you are ready, you can send your resume out to a few of those companies," her aunt suggested.

"That's what I thought too," she agreed, and they continued to discuss Charlie's career and the opportunities it afforded while they visited.

"By this time next year, I should have *that* paid off." She nodded towards the Miata. "Then, I can plan on getting a townhome."

"Why not a house?"

"Do you know how expensive houses are in Massachusetts?"

Nodding, they continued their conversation, passing the time until Charlie reluctantly announced she had to be going. "Mom is going to be expecting me."

"Well, don't you leave town without coming for another visit," her aunt warned her, always pleased to spend time with the young woman.

"Bye, Aunt Kitty. You behave now," she warned the elderly woman with a smile as she hugged and kissed her. Then, she looked at old Roy-Boy and said, "You take care of her, ya hear?" The elderly dog thumped his tail on the porch as though he understood every word. He even gave her a slight, "Woof," in agreement. The other three dogs looked on expectantly. "Behave yourselves," Charlie teased as she signaled to Cara that they were going. The well-behaved Poodle trotted down the steps with Charlie, her tail waving in the air and making it look as though she were sashaying towards the car. Charlie opened the door for the dog, who hopped into the front seat and proudly took her place. She looked back laughingly at the other dogs as Charlie replaced the Doggles over her eyes. "Bye," Charlie called once more as she got behind the wheel and waved.

Kitty waved until the car was out of sight and then smiled as she remembered the conversation, treasuring every moment until she would hear from her beloved niece again.

TO BE CONTINUED...

About the Author

K'Anne Meinel is a Lesbian Fiction bestselling author with more than 100 published works including shorts, novellas, and novels. She is an American author born in Milwaukee, Wisconsin and raised in Oconomowoc. Upon early graduation from high school she went to a private college in Milwaukee and then moved to California for seventeen years before returning to the state. Many of her stories have Wisconsin in them as settings for her wonderful, realistic, and detailed backgrounds. Named the lesbian Danielle Steel of her time, K'Anne continues to write interesting stories in a variety of genres in both the lesbian and mainstream fiction categories.

What do you do when you meet someone who changes everything you know about love and passion?

Paige Harlow is a good girl. She's always known where she was going in life: top grades, an ivy league school, a medical degree, regular church attendance, and a happy marriage to a man. So falling in love with her gorgeous roommate and best friend Alyssa Torres is no small crisis. Alyssa is chasing demons of her own, a medical condition that makes her an outcast and a family dysfunctional to the point of disintegration make her a questionable choice for any stable relationship. But Paige's heart is no longer her own. She must now battle the prejudices of her family, friends, and church and come to peace with her new sexuality before she can hope to win the affections of the woman of her dreams. But will love be enough?

When Delaney Delacroix is called to locate a missing girl, she never plans on getting caught up with a human trafficking investigation or with the local witch. Meeting with Raelin Montrose changes her life in so many ways that Delaney isn't sure that this isn't destiny.

Raelin Montrose is a practicing Wiccan, and when the ley lines that run under her home tell her that someone is coming, she can't imagine that she was going to solve a mystery and find the love of her life at the same time.

www.shadoepublishing.com

~ Because a publisher should stand behind their authors~

Amelia Gittens had the credit of being the first and only woman thus far in the United States military of being a sniper in combat, made possible by being in the Military Police unit of the crack 10th Mountain Infantry Division. After retirement she joins the City of New York Police Department, and suddenly finds herself involved in a suspect shooting incident which soon encroaches upon her entire life. In order to protect her therapist who has been targeted as a revenge killing, Amelia takes on the responsibility as if she was still in the Army, treating it as a tactical maneuver.

 *~ Because a publisher should stand behind their authors~*

An abused and bullied teenager is suddenly granted great and terrible powers by an ancient goddess. Each step towards womanhood is shaped by her new abilities, as is the woman she will become. Devil or angel, which will she be? Will the woman who chases her ever know for sure?

Both men tried to shoot her then, and the two women were stunned at the speed with which she moved. Penny charged straight at the gunmen then dove under their fire. Spinning on her back she kicked the legs from under one man, and as he fell, she kicked the gun from the other man's hand. Spinning back to the first man she saw the gun barrel moving toward her, and she lashed out with her foot. Her boot crushed his skull and she rolled to her feet to grab the last man in a neck lock. A quick twist and he lay lifeless in her arms.

She let him fall, as, breathing deeply, she came down off combat mode. "Are you ladies all right?" she asked as she untied the ropes that held the older woman.

"Who are you?" asked the old woman fearfully, as she pulled the tape from her mouth.

"They call me Lady Blue," smiled Penny as she helped the woman to stand.

"What are you?" It was the younger woman who spoke.

"Cold, hungry, dead tired, and covered in blue war paint," giggled Penny as she released the older woman's arm. She turned and began to search the bodies.

www.ingramcontent.com/pod-product-compliance
Lightning Source LLC
Chambersburg PA
CBHW070758120626
46557CB00002B/649